Natasha was galloping  ~~ shoulder, "There may be

She could see that the level crossing gates were big Clydesdale had his qu grazed the bank. Misty, t beside the rails. The fence ...een the field and the line lay a tangled heap of wire, surrounded by bits of paper and old bottles. The other horses grazed the banks, oblivious of danger.

Also by Christine Pullein-Thompson

Christine Pullein-Thompson

PONY PATROL
Fights Back

Illustrated by Jennifer Bell

SIMON & SCHUSTER
YOUNG BOOKS

Text copyright © 1977 Christine Pullein-Thompson
Illustrations copyright © 1992 Jennifer Bell
Cover photograph by Rowan Isaac

First published in Great Britain in 1977
by Dragon Books
This edition published in 1992
by Simon & Schuster Young Books

Photoset in North Wales by
Derek Doyle & Associates, Mold, Clwyd.
Printed and bound in Great Britain by
The Guernsey Press Co. Ltd, Guernsey, Channel Islands

Simon & Schuster Young Books
Campus 400
Maylands Avenue
Hemel Hempstead HP2 7EZ

British Library Cataloguing in Publication Data available

ISBN 0 7500 0809 1
ISBN 0 7500 0810 5 (pb)

Contents

Chapter One

The Patrol meets again

Marvin pedalled into the yard, his red hair on end, yelling, "William, where are you? We've been burgled! Everything's gone."

William straightened his back. He had been picking out the Clydesdale's hoofs. There was sunlight in his eyes and the smell of spring in his nostrils. Hens scratched with tiny chicks imitating them, their legs like matchsticks, working like clockwork.

"When did it happen?" he asked.

He was tall and lean and always working. Behind him was the house where he lived – a comfortable, rambling, inconvenient farmhouse.

"We've been away. Mum and Dad were in Paris for a week. I was with my cousins. When we came back the place was in ruins. The colour telly has gone, all the silver, my stereo, everything. They've even slashed mattresses looking for money. And to cap it all, they took it all away in Dad's brand new Rover," finished Marvin, still puffing with dismay.

"Have you told the police?"

"Of course. They're looking for fingerprints, going over the whole place now. There's a gang going round burgling all the empty houses. Ours is just one of many to them. They could do you next."

"They'll never burgle us," replied William.

"Why?"

"Because we never go away and because we haven't anything worth stealing; even our car is ten years old," replied William.

"Mum's in tears. They had a meal in the kitchen and left their dirty plates on the table for us to wash up. It's awful, it really is. We've got to catch them, William."

Marvin's asthma was coming on. He could feel his throat growing tight.

"What about Skinflint?" asked William.

"He came with me, because my cousins ride too. It's the first holiday any of us have had in years; it's so unfair."

"I suppose you did all the wrong things, left messages for the milkman saying, 'back in five days' and another for the paperboy," said William.

"Yes, we did actually," replied Marvin, looking ashamed. "And we left the key under a flower pot, so they just opened the door and walked straight in. We made all the mistakes. I'm not pretending we didn't."

"So what do you want?" asked William.

"The Patrol to help to catch them, to bring the burglars to justice. I'd like to kill them," said Marvin, wringing his hands. "I would really."

"Call a meeting then, call everyone," cried William, with a sudden feeling of mounting excitement. "Do you want to meet here?"

"Yes please, our place is chaos and Mum can't stop crying."

"Do you want to use our phone?"

"Yes please, ours doesn't work any more. Nothing works, they smashed everything up. It's awful, it really is."

They left their boots in the back porch. William's mother was in the kitchen. "What is it now?" she asked.

"Marvin's place has been burgled. The Patrol is in action again," said William. "We're going to catch the thieves."

"Oh dear," cried Mrs Gaze. "Your poor parents, Marvin. Can we lend you anything? Sit down a minute. I'll make you some tea. You look completely washed out."

"I am," said Marvin gratefully.

"Sit down, just push the cat off the chair. You do the telephoning, William, Marvin's all in," said Mrs Gaze.

"I wonder why I always have to do everything," muttered William, going towards the telephone. "I never have a minute's peace, it's William here, William there, all day long." But even as he muttered he was seeing the Patrol riding forth in action again. We need to find the empty houses first, then watch them. It won't be easy, he thought. Thank goodness the holidays have started.

Amanda was cleaning Tango's tack in the kitchen, when William telephoned.

"Come right away; it's urgent," William said. "Ride over if you like, but come."

"What's happened?" she asked.

"Marvin's been burgled. We've got to catch the thieves," answered William, putting down the receiver.

Alison was cleaning the sitting room when the

phone rang. She answered efficiently saying, "This is Ashworth 646220, who's calling?"

"It's William. Can you come over? The Patrol is in action again," he replied.

"What for?"

"Burglary. Can you come?"

"Okay. I'll bike, it's quicker than coming on Rainbow. I'll have to leave a message for Mum," she said, her brain tearing ahead.

"Okay, but come!" he cried, ringing off.

He imagined them gathering together again, facing danger as they had in the past – riding against arsonists, looking for a lost child, bringing horses away from flood and starvation. Remembering made his blood race.

Who next? he thought.

"Shall I try Natasha?" he called to Marvin who was still drinking tea in the kitchen.

"If you like."

Natasha was beautiful, highly strung, and very rich compared to the rest of them. She was washing her hair when he telephoned.

"Of course I'll come," she said, her hair dripping water on to the hall carpet. "I'll come on my scooter. I'll just dry my hair first. But what's happened?"

"Burglary and theft," he answered.

"Can I bring Michael?"

"Who's he?"

"A friend."

"Can he be trusted?"

"Of course. His father owns a garage. He's been burgled too."

"What about transport?"

"He's got a scooter too."

"Well, tell him to leave his guns at home," said William, remembering an incident from the past.

"Shall I ring the younger members?" asked William, going into the kitchen. "There's six of us now."

"Not yet then," Marvin answered. "They'll only fall off and get in the way, and it may be dangerous. The police say there's a gang doing it, not just one or two. You need to be at least fourteen to fight back effectively."

His breathing was normal now. Mrs Gaze had gone back to her cooking. Sunlight showed up the dust on the old-fashioned chimney piece above the ancient Aga.

"First we must find the empty houses; then watch them," William said, pouring himself tea.

"We won't be able to watch them day and night," Marvin replied.

"No, we'll have to do spot checks, back up the police who will be watching them too. Thank God Boxer is sound again," replied William.

"How are the horses we rescued?" asked Marvin.

"Okay. They look quite different. We're keeping the Clydesdale to work on the farm and Riding for the Disabled is probably taking the dun and the bay pony; and I'm hoping to Point-to-Point the grey. We traced her history. She won a few races five years back; and you know my passion for greys."

"And when they came they could hardly stagger," remembered Marvin.

They could hear hoofs now. "It must be Amanda," William said, going outside.

She was riding Tango, who was fat and sleek and shining.

11

"What's going on, for goodness sake?" she called.

"We've been burgled," Marvin called.

Presently they were all assembled. Alison arrived last. Natasha's friend Michael was tall and slim with hair greased back and a T-shirt which said *Alfa Romeo* on the front. "Hi," he said. "Nice to meet you."

William didn't trust him, not yet anyway. "Have you got a horse?" he asked.

"Yeah, three. I jump," he said.

"What, BSJA?" asked Amanda.

"Yeah, that's it."

"When were you burgled?" asked William.

"Ten days ago. They took all the day's takings and a lot of tyres. It wasn't funny, I'm telling you," he said.

He had clear, cool, grey eyes and an accent which sounded Australian.

"He's all right," said Natasha, smiling at him with her green eyes. "I promise."

She took off her helmet and shook her hair.

Amanda always felt ordinary beside her, plain and down-to-earth, like a cob standing alongside an Anglo-Arab. Alison was somewhere between the two. Always tidy with never a button missing, she was slim with blue eyes and short neat hair. William had never really trusted Natasha, but he trusted Amanda completely.

"Let's begin," he said now. "There are chairs in the front of the house."

Amanda had put Tango in one of the loose boxes. The scooters were leaning against the wall, the sun was still shining and somewhere a hen was cackling proudly about the egg she had just laid.

"I've read about your exploits in the press," said Michael, following William. "But I never thought I would have the honour of joining you."

"We're proud to have you actually," said Natasha quickly.

Everything was growing, the grass, the young calves, the foal they had brought back from the marshes more dead than alive; even themselves without knowing it.

Marvin remembered two hours ago when his mother was screaming in the kitchen and his father was running for the nearest phone. It had seemed an endless nightmare. He had gone from room to room, looking for his stereo equipment. He simply couldn't believe that they had lost so much. Now he felt calmer. He was seeing things in better perspective, but he was still angry, still saying to himself, "Why should they get away with it?"

Michael was genuinely pleased to be there. He liked the look of everybody and he liked the atmosphere.

Alison was liking him, liking his eyes and the way he talked, while Amanda was still trying to sum him up, to decide what sort of person he really was.

The front garden was small with a wall round it. It was rare for anyone to sit in it, because the Gazes hardly ever sat down anywhere for more than a few minutes unless it was to eat.

William found chairs and a bench. "Sit you down," he said, sounding like his mother. He found some paper and a pencil while they talked.

And his mother called to him, "Nothing dangerous this time, William. I can't stand any more accidents," as he went through the kitchen.

14

He answered glibly, "Don't worry, Mum, there won't be any." But he forgot to touch wood, which was something he remembered with regret later on.

"Okay?" he asked, sitting next to Amanda on the bench. "Here goes then." It was like a game, like a war planned on paper, no one had an inkling of what lay ahead. None of them questioned anything. It was just something exciting to do in the holidays to fill in the time, and there might be glory or simply failure.

No one imagined death or all the worry and horror to come. They felt as bright and as fearless as the spring sunshine.

Chapter Two

"Set a thief to catch a thief"

"We will make a list of the empty houses first. We can ride round tomorrow and look and report back," said William.

"How will we know they're empty?" asked Amanda. "Do we knock on the doors or guess? Some people may be out for the day."

"They are at risk too," said Michael. "Thieves learn your habits and then pounce."

"If everything is locked up, then the house is empty. Okay?" asked William.

"Better safe than sorry," agreed Marvin.

"I refuse to try doors," said Alison.

"Why not knock and introduce yourself?" asked Natasha with a dazzling smile. "Just say, 'I'm from the Pony Patrol, checking up'."

"Just play it by ear," said Michael.

"We don't want to look suspicious," muttered Alison.

"Exactly," agreed Amanda.

"I can tell when a house is empty. It looks empty. Perhaps I'm mad or something, but that's the way it looks," said William, exasperated. "There's no dog in the garden, the garage is locked, there's a give-away message left for the milkman; all the gates are firmly shut, the house is silent, and the flowers need watering."

"You'd make a good burglar," exclaimed Michael, smiling.

"Poachers make the best gamekeepers," replied William.

"Set a thief to catch a thief," said Marvin.

"Let's put an advertisement in the local paper, a big one on the back, something like: GOING AWAY? TELL THE PONY PATROL TO KEEP WATCH. FOR EFFICIENT SERVICE, RING dot dot dot and William's number," suggested Amanda.

"Fantastic," said Michael.

"Brilliant," cried Natasha.

"When's publication date?" asked Alison.

"Friday, and if we hand it in today it will just make it," said Amanda.

"If someone writes it, I'll deliver it on the way home," cried Natasha.

We're getting on, thought William; Michael's an asset and Amanda's marvellous as usual. They were all a little light-headed with excitement.

The girls were drafting the advertisement now. The air was full of enthusiasm.

"I'm so glad to be here," said Michael. 'I'm so glad we're fighting back."

"Same here," agreed William. And now they liked each other and it was like a sudden gift.

"I've learnt some judo," Michael said. "Not much, but enough."

The advertisement was done now. Natasha put it in her pocket.

"Let's get moving right away. Skinflint needs

exercising, and I can't bear being at home," Marvin said. "Which district shall I take?"

"We can't cover more than fifteen kilometres," answered William.

"And that's an awful lot," said Alison.

They concentrated on an ordnance survey map and divided the area up, each taking the area nearest home. They looked at each other and cried, "That's it then."

And Natasha said, "Michael and I can cover a fair bit on the way home."

"We will start officially tomorrow afternoon, okay?" asked William.

"Okay."

"We can't fail, can we? I mean you've never failed yet, have you?" asked Michael.

"There's always a first time," replied Amanda.

"And the end can be sticky," suggested William.

"And full of misery," added Marvin.

Another minute and the scooters were starting up with a roar, Tango's hoofs clattered on the concrete yard, and Alison slid away silently on her bike.

"Tomorrow here at twelve," yelled William. "Bring your lunches and your lists of empty houses."

"Sure," they yelled. "Goodbye." And the air was full of dust and their voices, until they and the hoofbeats and the roar of engines had faded away.

"What are you up to now?" asked Mrs Gaze as William went through the kitchen.

"Nothing much."

"You're plotting something."

"Not really."

He put on his boots and went to see Boxer, who

had the head of a hunter and the heart of a lion and was fifteen two and a gelding.

"We're back in harness, old fellow," he said. "We're on the warpath again." He felt Boxer's old grey legs; they were cool and clean, with no lumps anywhere.

"It's burglars this time," he said. "A gang, but we'll beat them between us." Boxer nuzzled his pockets and rubbed his nose against his sleeve and William said, "You're the best, there's no other horse can beat you." He pictured them galloping after burglars with the moon in the sky and somewhere a bird calling, and he thought, we're going to win again, we're going to get Marvin's things back, no matter what. Now he was impatient to begin, to be out watching and waiting, to be really living again. It's like waiting for a hunt to begin, he thought, but this time it isn't sport – it's real!

"William's nice, isn't he?" cried Natasha, yelling above the noise of her scooter.

"They all are," shouted Michael.

They were nearly in the town now. Presently they parked their scooters and went to the printers. Natasha handed over the advertisement to a woman who had a snub nose, was wearing glasses, and had a perpetual sniff.

"Wait a minute," she sniffed. "I must show it to Mr Snagge."

Natasha took off her helmet, Michael lit a cigarette.

"You'll die. Cigarettes kill; they give you cancer, you fool," said Natasha.

The woman came back with a small man with a moustache.

19

"Is this all right?" he said. "You know what you're doing?"

"Ring my dad if you like," said Michael. "You must know him, Jim Gilbey, Hilltop Motors. He'll give you the okay."

Natasha pulled out her purse and smiled and said, "How much is it, please?"

"I've heard of the Pony Patrol of course," said Mr Snagge.

"That's all right then," replied Natasha politely. "We just want to help people, that's all."

"That's five pounds then," said Mr Snagge.

They paid and laughed all the way to the Hilltop Motors, which smelt of petrol. There was a dump of old cars beyond the petrol pumps and Michael's three horses standing head to tail, their coats gleaming in the sunlight.

"We forgot to look for empty houses," said Natasha.

"So we did," replied Michael. "But don't worry, I've got to ride my horses yet. I'll ride them three different ways and keep looking."

"See you tomorrow then. We go mounted because it's a pony patrol," replied Natasha.

"Trouble is mine are all horses. I'll take Bouncer, he's the smallest, but he still isn't a pony," said Michael, laughing.

"It doesn't matter," said Natasha.

She didn't want to go. She liked Michael because he was uncomplicated. He didn't try to be anyone; he was just himself.

"Be seeing you then," she said at last.

Michael's father was in the office arguing with a customer. When he had finished, Michael said, "I've joined the Pony Patrol, Dad. They're a great crowd."

His father didn't ask questions, just said, "Well done, son," and that was that.

Natasha's parents were out when she reached home, but Nanny was there complaining loudly. "You're always out. You've been with that boy from the garage again, haven't you?"

Natasha screamed, "So what?" and rushed upstairs, slamming her bedroom door after her. She could hear Nanny calling, "Your father wouldn't like it. You'll go to the bad like your brother. You mark my words. You'll come to a bad end."

Amanda turned Tango into the tiny paddock at the side of the bungalow where she lived and darted indoors.

"Lunch is all dried up," her mother said. "Why are you so late?"

"The Pony Patrol is in action again. Marvin's cottage has been burgled. We've got to help, they've lost everything. I'm sorry Mum,' replied Amanda.

"I won't have you hurt," her mother said. "You've suffered enough. Let someone else bear the burden this time."

"They helped me find Tango, and we caught the arsonist who was burning William's straw, so we've *got* to help Marvin. Can't you understand?" pleaded Amanda.

"You're a girl. Leave it to the boys. You could have died last time," said her mother, heaping two plates with stewed lamb.

"Marvin helped me so I'm helping him, it's as simple as that," replied Amanda. "Do you know anyone who's gone away on holiday?"

'Well, there's Mr and Mrs Holsworthy," said her mother after a pause, "they've got a lovely place. Now what's it called? Let me see, Jacky's Mill, I think. They've gone to Venice. They said it smelt less in the spring."

"Oh Mum, you're marvellous," cried Amanda, swallowing stew. "Anyone else?"

"Well, Yew Tree Cottage is empty at the moment. I think the furniture's gone, but it might be worth investigating."

"I could do that on foot, straight after lunch," said Amanda happily. "Oh Mum, you're wonderful."

Alison's home was small and untidy. Her mother was out when she returned. There was a note on the table which read, "Lunch in the fridge", and a smell of gas in the kitchen.

Her dun pony Rainbow saw her and whinnied. She left the back door open and took him a handful of pony cubes.

"We're in action again," she told him. "We're fighting again."

Suddenly the empty house and the loneliness didn't matter so much. "I'm just going to eat lunch and then we're looking for deserted houses," she told Rainbow. "And tomorrow we're riding with William and a new boy called Michael and a couple of girls," and she knew she was happy again.

She turned the radio on and listened to it as she ate her lunch. There was a shipwreck off Norway and fighting in the Middle East, but none of it really sank into her brain, because all the time she was making plans, hoping that she and William would patrol together, picturing them hacking along country roads at twilight. I don't want to ride with Marvin, she thought; Michael might be all right – he looks as though he could fight!

Marvin's mother was still crying. The police had gone and his father had put off going to work.

The ripped mattresses were neatly stacked by the dustbins. Inside the cottage was nearly back to normal, though it looked very bare with no silver ornaments on the table in the sitting room, and no television.

"Where have you been, Marvin? Why didn't you stay and help?" asked his mother.

"I've summoned the Patrol," replied Marvin.

"What Patrol?" demanded his father.

"The Pony Patrol."

"You're mad," replied his mother. "What good can *they* do?"

"Plenty," said Marvin.

His mother hid her face in her hands. "Nothing will ever bring back my treasures," she said.

Marvin could feel his asthma coming back. "Is there any lunch?" he asked.

"Lunch? Who wants lunch?" cried his mother.

"I'm going to the pub to get some. I was just waiting for you," his father said.

Marvin went outside to Skinflint who was restless, because he was missing the ponies he had been staying with.

I must keep calm, thought Marvin. If I keep calm my asthma will go away. Birds were singing in the trees and suddenly for a second, he wished he owned nothing, like a bird, nothing which could be taken away from him. Then he remembered their nests and how they were robbed, and he didn't want to be a bird any more. His father was calling to him now, saying, "Coming to the pub with me, Marvin? You can have a drink outside." And he started to feel better.

Life goes on. We can exist without colour telly and silver ornaments, he thought. And my stereo was old and well-used.

"The trees are all in blossom," his father said.

"The Patrol is going to catch them, Dad," he said. "I promise that."

"I'm so glad," replied his father. "I'm sure they will too." But Marvin knew he didn't mean it. He was just saying it to be pleasant, to jolly him along. But we'll show them, thought Marvin. We'll catch them somehow and teach the villains a lesson.

"Is Skinflint all right?" asked his father, trying to be pleasant again.

"Fine, except for missing his friends," said Marvin.

Chapter Three

Pigs

"Dad's got a photocopier, so I've had copies made of the local ordnance survey map," said Michael, riding into the yard on dark brown Bouncer. "We can mark the empty houses with an X."

Amanda was already there on anglo-arab Tango. They could see dun Rainbow and Alison in the distance, and Boxer stood ready tacked up in a loose box. It was another fine day.

"Well done," said William.

"Let's get down to marking the houses then. I've found two," announced Amanda.

"Here comes Marvin," said Michael.

"I've only found one and it's a pretty humble one with the paint peeling off the walls and neighbours on each side and a garden full of weeds," said William.

Amanda was marking her empty houses on the maps. Michael added two more – "One's superb, full of sculptures; the other's only a cottage, but it's got some nice pictures which might be worth a bit," he said. He felt one hundred per cent alive today, and ready for anything.

William stood admiring Bouncer, who had well

let-down hocks, a wise head and sensible, round hoofs.

Alison was marking the map now. "Mine aren't very expensive houses," she said, "but the dustbins have been put out three days early for collection, so I reckon the owners must be away."

"I've found one with a note for the milkman. It's at the end of a lane," said Marvin, sliding off Skinflint's back.

"Is Natasha always late?" asked Michael, impatient to be off. "How long do we have to wait?"

"A little longer," replied William.

"I've got two horses to school when I get home, or Dad will be furious," Michael said.

Natasha came at last, looking immaculate, on her prancing speckled mare, Checked Princess. "Sorry I'm late. Mum returned from London unexpectedly."

"Did you find any empty houses?" called William.

"I didn't have time to look."

Michael was handing the maps round. "That makes eight empty houses altogether," he said.

"We're just having a hack round today. Tomorrow we'll be more serious. You may want to cross mine off," William said.

"And mine," said Alison.

The horses liked each other's company. Blossom blew from the trees into their manes.

"I've brought my grandad's binoculars. He had them in the war; he always called them 'his field glasses'. They're pretty good. If we stop I think I can see two of the empty houses from here, your two, Amanda," said William.

He drew rein and looked at the one called Jacky's Mill; it had a large van outside.

"Action stations!" he cried. "There's a van outside Jacky's Mill. Gallop."

None of them was prepared for such immediate action. A wide straight road lay ahead with grass verges. They gave their horses their heads.

"It's one o'clock. No one burgles at one o'clock,' cried Alison.

"How do you know?" cried Amanda.

"I feel it in my bones."

"They're pretty useless bones then," shouted Michael, laughing with excitement.

They were clattering past other houses now, past Amanda's home, past dreamy, empty Yew Tree Cottage. The horses were pulling, racing each other.

There was just a short bit of empty road and a bridge now between them and Jacky's Mill.

"Amanda take the van number, because you've got a good memory. Alison look at the men's faces. Natasha get your charm switched on," said William. "Michael be ready to dial 999."

Two men were coming out of Jacky's Mill. There was a bird bath in the garden and roses everywhere and the sweet sickly smell of hyacinths.

The van had "Electrocaire" written on it. William halted Boxer. He wasn't sure what to say. Then Natasha spoke.

"Excuse me, is anyone at home?" she asked.

"No one, love," said one of the men. "We're just putting the washing machine in order."

"How did you get in then?" asked Michael.

"Through the door, mate." They were large men in overalls.

They started to get into the van.

27

"But the door shouldn't be open," cried Amanda. "The people are away."

The men were laughing now. "What are you playing at then? Being detectives, are you?" they asked.

"That's right," replied William. "We're checking up."

"And we want to see what's in your van," cried Michael brazenly.

"Well, so you shall," replied the elder man, getting out. "Anything to please."

He opened the van doors and there was nothing but a bag of tools inside. "Satisfied?" he asked.

"Yes, thank you," said Alison.

"And the home help's inside, if you want to make sure," the man said, chuckling.

"I feel such a fool," cried Amanda as the van disappeared with the men still laughing inside.

"We're sure to make mistakes," said William.

"It won't 'alter the fate of nations'," quoted Marvin, which was what his father said constantly to his mother.

"We must work out a plan," said Michael. "A way of tackling things."

"That's easier said than done," replied Alison.

"I still feel awful," said Amanda.

"I feel a fool," said William.

" 'He who makes no mistakes, makes nothing'," quoted Marvin.

"They were sweet really. They took it as a joke. It made their day," said Natasha, laughing. "For goodness sake why can't we laugh at ourselves?

William was looking at the map. "There's The Laurels next. That's one of yours, Alison," he said.

29

"Okay, let's get going mates," cried Michael, pretending to ride like a jockey.

"It's a gloomy sort of house, but it might have riches inside," said Alison.

"Any cars?" asked Michael.

"I didn't look. It's the sort of place where cats lurk under bushes, and nothing has been altered for fifty years."

They were trotting now and the horses were excited again.

"They think they're hunting," William said.

"And they're right in a way," said Amanda.

"Let's have lunch soon," suggested Marvin. "My stomach's rumbling."

"What are we going to do if there's a van outside again?" asked Amanda.

"Creep round the back of the house and peep through the windows," replied Michael.

"Supposing we're caught? If the police are keeping an eye on the place they could think we were the burglars," said Alison.

"We're nearly there," replied William. "Stop fussing."

The house stood alone on a bend in the road. There was no car in sight.

"I'll just peep through the windows," Michael said. "Hold Bouncer someone."

The trees grew up to the windows. Alison took Bouncer.

"I hope we can eat soon, I'm starving," Marvin said.

Michael climbed a tree and peered through a window.

"It's flipping empty," he called.

"How was I to know?" asked Alison.

30

"It doesn't matter," said William.

"Let's eat now," said Marvin.

They let their horses graze a grass verge while they ate.

"We're not getting anywhere," Marvin said.

"Yes we are, this is only the beginning," replied Amanda.

"There's a horse show next week and I'm entered," said Alison.

"And I'm going to an indoor jumping show. I want to upgrade Black Tulip," said Michael.

"We can go on without you," William replied. "We can rope in some younger people. I'm putting *this* first. I want to catch the gang. You don't seem to care."

He started to pull up Boxer's girths. The sunshine had gone. Dark clouds glowered over them. Soon it would rain.

"Let's go," he said, mounting.

"I'm still eating," grumbled Marvin. "You gobbled."

"Busy people always do," replied William.

Nearly a kilometre away stood another of Alison's houses. It had wrought-iron gates and was red brick with 1869 carved above the front door.

"It's certainly empty," William said.

"We had better go round the back," replied Michael, jumping off Bouncer.

"I'll go with you since it's my house," cried Alison.

Spots of rain were falling now. The house stood stark and alone among ploughed fields. The two of them vanished round the far side of the house.

"There's plenty of tyre marks," Amanda said, peering at the ground. "Don't you think we should bring magnifying glasses like real detectives?"

"Yes. And other things like gloves so we don't destroy their fingerprints," said Marvin.

Michael and Alison were coming back now. Michael's voice was shaking.

"It's been done," he said.

"What do you mean?" cried William.

"Go and have a look."

"It's awful! They've ruined it; they've spoilt everything. They must be totally evil," said Alison, wiping her eyes. "I can't bear such destruction."

William was running towards the house now, but Marvin hadn't moved. "I don't want to see it," he said in a miserable voice.

"It's worse than your house. It must be," replied Alison.

Amanda followed William. Together they peered through the windows. Pictures had been ripped off the walls and smashed. Chair covers ripped. There were smashed bottles everywhere, broken glasses and PIGS scrawled in red paint across the walls. Beautiful china plates lay smashed. Electric sockets had been ripped off walls, books torn to shreds.

"Let's go back, let's ring the police," said William.

"What sort of people are they?" asked Amanda, shuddering. "I don't understand."

"Swine is too nice a word for them," said William.

He mounted Boxer saying, "There's a telephone kiosk a kilometre back, let's go." Now it was raining in earnest.

None of them felt like talking. It was as though they were facing reality for the first time. They knew now what they were up against and it sent a cold shiver down their spines.

"I'm not going to the jumping show after all; I don't care what Dad says. This is more important," said Michael after a time.

"Same here," said Alison.

William dialled 999. "What was the house called?" he yelled, opening the kiosk door.

"New Lodge," shouted Alison.

The police were quick and efficient.

"We needn't stay, need we?" asked William.

"No. You say you're the Pony Patrol. Where can I find you?" asked the voice at the other end of the line.

William gave his own telephone number. "They're sending two police cars straight away. They don't need us," he said.

They were all soaking wet now but they hardly noticed.

"I think we should call it a day," said Natasha. "I'm glad I didn't look. I can't bear to see beautiful things smashed."

"They are the sort of things which are irreplaceable," said Alison. "And the couple who live there are quite old. I'm so terribly sorry for them."

She was blowing her nose. "I remember them quite well now. They're kind of stately, as though they've known better days."

"That's why they called them PIGS," said William.

They were cantering along a grass verge without really noticing. William was wondering what would happen if they ever came face to face with the gang. Natasha was imagining her own home in ruins. There were two burglar alarms, but would that be enough? she wondered.

Marvin was imagining PIGS scrawled across his bedroom walls in red paint while Alison saw the stately couple weeping in her mind's eye. They'll never be the same again, she thought. The shock could kill them.

Amanda was wondering about the gang – why did they do it? Why did they hate so much? What did they look like? How could they live with so much evil inside them?

Michael was angry. He wanted to meet the gang face to face, to smash them with his bare hands. He knew how hard his father had worked for what he had now. What if all that was smashed? All those years of work gone in a few hours!

"They're the pigs," he yelled.

"Don't insult pigs, please," shouted William.

"I'd like to kill them," shouted Michael. "And by God I mean it."

The wind and the rain blew in their faces and the clouds sank lower, but none of them noticed, for each of them was picturing the future ahead, the long battle, the early mornings and the late nights until at last they met the thieves face to face.

"We won't give up," shouted William.

"Never," yelled Amanda.

"They could be our friends," said Alison.

"Not likely," said Marvin.

"My brother's friends," replied Natasha.

"That's quite possible," declared Alison.

"Your brother can't be that idiotic," shouted William.

And the horses sensed their mood and were filled with excitement; they tossed their heads and raced each other and presently two cars came by full of grim-faced policemen, and William waved and shouted, "Good luck! Catch the villains! Lock them up!"

They all felt a little mad and light-headed because they had found something and the struggle was beginning.

I feel as though a great battle is about to begin, thought William.

I'm so glad I'm here, thought Michael.

What will we find next? wondered Amanda.

How could they do it? Alison asked herself.

Natasha wondered what they looked like and whether they wore masks. Now they had reached the parting of their ways. Marvin looked at the landscape and tried not to think at all.

"We had better start earlier tomorrow. How about five a.m.?" asked William.

"Make it four," answered Michael.

"I'll never make it," complained Natasha.

"I'll give you a buzz," said Michael.

"Nanny will be furious."

"Forget Nanny. Who wants a nanny at your age, anyway?" asked Michael.

"I'm stuck with her," said Natasha.

William rode homewards well satisfied with the day's events. The roads were wet with rain and you could almost feel the grass growing. Boxer wasn't tired, but walked with the long swinging stride which meant he was happy. Tomorrow! I wish it was here already he thought. I shall never sleep tonight and, if I do, I shall dream of the gang.

"About time too," called his father as he entered the farmyard. "How about helping with the milking?"

"All right, I'm coming," shouted William.

Suddenly it was like any other day, except that it was lit by the light of suspense and in the back of his mind he was waiting for the battle to begin.

Chapter Four

"A kind of blackmail"

Nothing happened on the next day. The thieves seemed to have gone to ground. The empty houses stood undisturbed and the Patrol added one more to their list, a modern one with diamond panes and an ornamental wishing well.

Its owner had left a note for the milkman saying, *"Away for a week. Milk again on Friday."*

Marvin wanted to tear the note up; but Amanda insisted that the milkman must see it first, or the owners would come back to no milk. The house had a burglar alarm, and the windows looked securely locked.

"I expect they'll give that one a miss anyway," said Alison.

After yesterday the whole of the day was an anticlimax, and the next day was no better. Natasha was grumbling by this time. "I can't keep getting up at the crack of dawn. Why don't we do it the other way round; set out at midnight?" she asked.

"You know our parents won't stand for it," replied Amanda. "They don't mind us rising early, but staying out all night is different, goodness knows why."

"My mother would go dotty; she's fed up with me now," said Alison. "I'm supposed to do the shopping, not to mention the housework. If you could hear the rows we've had!"

Later they stopped at a newsagent to buy the local paper. Their advertisement was on the back. "It looks fantastic," cried Michael. "Just look!"

"Now we'll get some calls," cried Amanda.

"I'd better go home," said William.

"We've drawn a blank anyway," agreed Marvin. 'And Skinflint could do with a break.''

The horses had had enough. William's mother met them at the farm entrance. "The police have been," she said.

"About the burgled house?" asked William.

"No, about your advertisement," replied his mother, looking worried. "They don't like it at all. They think you're sticking your necks out. They want you to stay at home. I'm sorry, but there it is."

"But we can't," cried Marvin. "We've got to have our revenge."

"Revenge is never a good motive," she said.

"I'm not giving up, and my dad's behind me," cried Michael. "He's said so."

"Well what about your mum?"

"She left years ago," said Michael.

"We must help Marvin. He's part of the Patrol. We want to get his things back, and quick," cried William.

"I want them sentenced to years and years in prison. You should see my Mum, she's gone to pieces since the burglary," cried Marvin, "and Dad is still waiting for another car. Everything was under-insured. I can promise you none of us is ever going on holiday again, we wouldn't dare."

"And look what they did to that old couple's house," cried Alison. "Why should they go scot-free? They're worse than animals. Much, much worse."

"The police can't stop us," said Natasha quietly. "There's no law against riding at night. If they want us to have lights, we can buy stirrup lights."

"And if we start at five a.m., it isn't even dark," added William.

They were getting off their horses now, feeling like troopers, like a proper horse patrol.

"The police can get stuffed as far as I'm concerned," exclaimed Michael. "And Dad would say the same. They spend all their time prosecuting motorists for exceeding the speed limit, instead of hunting thieves. I am going on, even if I go it alone."

"Same here," cried Alison.

"Here, here," shouted Marvin. "Up the Pony Patrol."

"To the end; the bitter end," cried Amanda.

"And it probably will be bitter," said William, depressed by the sight of his mother, in her down-at-heel slippers with her hair awry, and her face wrinkled with worry.

"We'll be all right, Mum. I promise," he said.

"You always say that. You've had one brush with thieves and ended up in hospital. And this time it could be fatal," she answered wearily.

"This will be the last time," said William.

"It had better be; I can't take much more and there goes the phone," she replied, hurrying away.

"It's started already. I bet you a hundred pounds

it's for the Pony Patrol," shouted William, running after her.

"Don't be so ridiculous," she said. "But answer it if you like."

"William Gaze here," he said.

"Is that the Pony Patrol?" asked a prim voice and he could have cried with delight.

"Yes, speaking."

"I'm away for five days next week. I've told the police, but will you keep an eye on the place too?"

"With pleasure, madam," answered William. "Can I have your address please?"

He wrote it down, his hand shaking with excitement.

"Now you won't leave any giveaway messages for the milkman, will you, or a window open for your cat?" he asked.

"No. Pussy has gone to a cattery and I've told the milkman by word of mouth," replied the prim voice.

"We'll do our best then. We can't be there all the time, but we will visit it personally once a day," promised William. "And on second thoughts, we'll watch it through binoculars, too, because one of our members lives quite near."

"How much do you charge?"

"Nothing, we do it for the good of the community," answered William, ringing off before she could say thank you.

He rushed out into the yard, crying, "It's begun. We've got our first customer and the house is quite near – Amanda and I can watch it through binoculars and phone you if we see anything and gallop forth. You could make it in time too, Marvin, but not Michael and Natasha, nor Alison. So out of hours we three will have to go it alone," said William.

"It's a beginning anyway," said Michael. "And the next one might be near me and Natasha. I think I'll buy some binoculars."

"I've got some opera glasses," said Natasha.

"There goes the telephone again," cried Marvin.

William answered again and a voice said, "Just leave us alone, see. Or you'll be sorry, that's the message. Get it?"

"No," shouted William. "Who are you?" But the caller had rung off and though he put the receiver back and waited, it didn't ring again.

He went back to the yard where the others still waited with their horses. The sun was shining again, making everything sparkle after the rain. He took hold of Boxer's reins and said, "It was them."

"Them?" cried Amanda. "Who's them?"

"The gang. They said if we don't stop our activities they are going 'to get us'," he said, and tried to imagine what "to get" meant to them and, remembering the stately couple's house, he was suddenly filled with the most frightening dread.

"We can't give in to threats," said Michael quietly.

"First it was the police who warned us, then them," replied William. "So we have been warned twice over. If anyone wants to give up now, there should be no recriminations, no scorn. We all have parents and animals and homes we love. We must think carefully, though I know already what my answer is – I go on."

"I too," shouted Michael.

"And I," shouted Marvin.

Alison and Amanda looked at one another.

41

Alison pictured the gang throwing acid in her face and making her ugly for ever. Amanda imagined her home burning, but deep down inside themselves, they were already saying, "Yes, yes to the very end."

"Me too," said Amanda.

"And me," added Alison.

"I can't say no," said Natasha slowly, "but you must realize how much there is at stake – our picture collection alone is worth a million. There are rugs worth thousands of pounds and first editions worth hundreds. But it's yes, a thousand times over. I couldn't let you go on without me."

"Don't tell your parents about the police and the threats. I can manage mine, but yours might not be so easy," advised William.

"I shall tell Dad about the burglaries and he can get a guard with an Alsatian or two. He can afford it. We can padlock the gates at night and put a notice up saying *Guard Dogs on Patrol* until we've caught them," replied Natasha.

"I hate threats," said Amanda.

"It's a kind of blackmail," said Alison.

"I'm scared. Don't you think we need weapons?" asked Amanda.

"No, not yet anyway," replied William. "If the police thought we were carrying guns they would go berserk."

He was untacking Boxer now automatically, like someone sleepwalking. "Let's meet at six tonight for a quick survey. Meanwhile Amanda and I will keep the new house in view through our binoculars," he said.

Another minute and the others were riding away talking to each other, imagining the worst that could happen. William turned Boxer out into the paddock behind the farmhouse. He felt as though he was walking a tightrope as he walked indoors; one false move and anything could happen. And they couldn't guard everybody, not themselves as well as all the empty houses.

His mother was ironing and said straight away, "I wish you would stop, William. I know your dad doesn't agree with me, but why stick out your neck for people you don't even know?"

Sadie, the old farm collie, licked his hand as though she knew what was coming to him and was comforting him in advance. He knelt down and she licked his face.

"If you weren't so old, you could come too," he said.

"You could be injured for life," his mother went on.

"We must fight for what we believe in. Anyway I shall be on Boxer and he'll see me through," replied William.

He could hear his father coming in now; the firm tread of his heavy boots and the smell of tobacco which always preceded him. And the sun was still shining. "We can't give up now," he said. "We're hot on their scent. It's like asking hounds to stop hunting in the middle of a run."

He went upstairs and looked through his binoculars at the prim lady's house, which was called Heron's Nest. Everything was quiet there with the daffodils just coming out and not a car to be seen anywhere. He could hear his parents talking on the landing below.

"He'd better go into the mounted police or the army; he's incurable," his father said.

"If only he doesn't get hurt," answered his mother.

And staring across the landscape, he knew he was afraid; he was scared of getting hurt, of being injured beyond repair, of physical pain, and he had never felt that way before. But he had been brought up to ignore fear, to walk past bellowing bulls and hold down unruly cows. He had been brought up to pretend bravery even when he didn't feel it, and he wasn't changing now. He said, for goodness sake William where's your courage, to himself, and shut the window and went downstairs. He told his mother that he would join the army with pleasure as soon as he was old enough; and he wished that they hadn't put the advertisement in the local paper after all, because it had alerted the thieves and now anything could happen.

Michael wasn't afraid. He liked the feeling of danger. He had wanted to be a speedway rider, to hurtle round a stadium on a motorcycle with danger facing him at every turn. He still dreamed of winning the Grand National. He rode home longing for a fight, thinking, we'll beat those swine, we'll teach them a lesson they'll never forget.

Meanwhile Natasha was trying to keep calm. She felt strung up, rather like a horse lining up at the start of a race. She felt as though she would never sleep properly again and yet she was too cowardly to back out, to face the others and say, "I'm giving up." It took less courage to go on.

Amanda was trying not to think about the thieves at all; she talked to Tango about oats and pony nuts and the shows which lay ahead, but all the time the feeling of fear was there, lurking in the back of her mind. Marvin was scared too, and when he was scared his asthma always started. He could feel his throat tightening and presently it spread to his chest. I must get home to my puffer, he thought, or I shall be useless tonight. And I can't miss tonight. If there's a fight, the others will need me. I must be well.

Alison was tired suddenly. She seemed to have been riding for hours and there was still tonight ahead. "I'll borrow one of William's horses. Otherwise I'll kill you, Rainbow," she said, patting his dun neck, and the day seemed to have lasted for years already and there was still the night to come.

Chapter Five

Poor Boxer!

It was four o'clock now. Alison had telephoned, asking to borrow a horse for the evening. "You can have Dad's old hunter, Mulberry," William had said. "He's huge, but kind and one hundred per cent trustworthy."

Alison had said that she would come at five to get him ready. Outside the cows were being milked and the sun had moved westwards, the yard was full of shadows.

But William wasn't looking at the yard, he was looking across flat fields to the Heron's Nest where there was something moving. He adjusted his grandfather's binoculars for the third time and now he could see two motor bikes and a van parked further down the road. His heart suddenly started pounding like a sledge hammer; then he was running downstairs, picking up the telephone and dialling Amanda's number. Her mother answered. "I need to speak to Amanda," he shouted. "It's urgent."

He heard Amanda running, calling, "Coming, Mum."

"There are people at the Heron's Nest," he said. "Telephone the others. I'm on my way."

"Be careful," she said.

He slammed down the receiver, ran for the stable where Boxer waited. He didn't want to lose a minute. He thought, if I can only catch a glimpse of them, or take the van number, it will be a beginning.

Boxer opened his mouth for the bit and William didn't stop for a saddle. He was used to riding bareback and he had to save time. He galloped out of the yard across the concrete, not sparing Boxer's legs, as his mother opened the back door and called, "Where are you going, William?"

He shouted, "Nowhere," because he couldn't think of anything else to say.

She went on calling, "William, William! Come back." But nothing could stop him now because his blood was up. He thought, there's none so deaf as those who do not wish to hear, and rode on.

A few kilometres away Marvin and Amanda were tacking up. Marvin's asthma had gone. He felt buoyed up with excitement. Ready for anything.

"This is it," he told chestnut Skinflint. "This is D day."

A mile away Amanda's mother called, "Shall I phone the police, Mandy? Wouldn't that be a good idea?" and Amanda yelled, "If you like, but don't dial 999 because it might be a false alarm." And then she was galloping through the garden gates on to the grass verge, thinking, if only we can be in time! Come on Tango, faster, faster! And the Heron's Nest was just a speck in the distance and the verge rough and full of ditches.

*

47

William was nearly there now. He could see everything plainly at last. There were four men altogether and their pockets were bulging with stolen goods. They wore gloves, and pulled masks over their faces as he drew near. They seemed to be expecting him and suddenly he was afraid. He halted Boxer and felt immensely vulnerable with out any weapon of any kind; he wanted armour suddenly, with a visor to protect his face and mailed gloves to protect his hands. The gang seemed to be smiling at him through their woollen masks.

They were all wearing motorbike gear – leather jackets, high boots, helmets. His old riding cap felt soft and useless by comparison, and he knew that Boxer was no match for their motorbikes. He was praying now that the others would come. And then without a word, the young men leapt on their motorbikes and with a great roar rode straight at him, swerving sideways at the last minute, missing him by less than an inch.

He rode Boxer into the side of the road but now they produced weapons – a piece of spiked fence, a wooden club, a bicycle chain. Boxer was losing his nerve and they were coming at him again, without speaking, with no noise but the roar of their motorbikes. Then something seemed to hit him and suddenly he was falling, and Boxer was falling too. He thought, if only the others would come. Where are they? Why don't they come?

Another minute and they had gone and there was blessed silence. He moved his legs and they still moved, and he licked his teeth and they were still there. Boxer stood over him, his grey coat stained with blood and now there were hoofs

coming along the road and from the other side a police car. He stood up and shouted, "You're too late! Why did you take so long?"

His neck felt wet and he thought, they got my face after all. Boxer had a gash right down his shoulder and he started to cry with an awful feeling of despair, and he hated the others for not coming in time, for taking so long.

Amanda slid off Tango, saying, "Oh my God!"

"We did our best," said Marvin, feeling sick at the sight of the blood, looking at Boxer and thinking, I bet they've severed a muscle, feeling a sort of sick fear, thanking God that it wasn't Skinflint.

The police got out of their car and said, "How are you, son?"

William pointed down the road and said, "They've gone that way. If you're quick you might catch them. There are four on motorbikes . . ."

His tears mixed with the blood and stung the wound on his face.

The police were sending for reinforcements as they ran for their cars and one of them yelled, "An ambulance?" And William shouted, "No thank you," and started to walk homewards along the road, leading Boxer. "I'm going home," he shouted. "I'm all right and I'm not giving up, not now or ever." His voice was strange and muffled because he was still crying, not for himself, but for Boxer.

"If only it could have been me this time. Everything always happens to William," said Amanda sadly.

"He should have waited," Marvin replied.

"He never would," replied Amanda. 'It's not in his character."

"Boxer will need stitching. He may be lame for life," said Marvin.

"Why did we get involved? Why? We should have listened to the police," cried Amanda. "It's their job after all."

"You got involved because of me," said Marvin.

"I'm not giving up, not now, not ever. Not after this," shouted William.

He could see the farm now. He didn't want to face his mother. He knew she would go on and on, saying, "I told you so. Why won't you listen?"

And the vet would have to come to stitch up Boxer.

He started to walk slower and slower and the others caught up with him and peered into his face and said, "Are you all right?"

"Fine," he answered.

"Well you don't look it," replied Amanda.

"If you think I'm going to pack it in because of today," said William, "you're wrong. I want my revenge now. I'm never giving up."

His mother was waiting outside the farmhouse peering anxiously along the drive. She waved and called, "Are you all right?" and then started to run towards him as he shouted, "Yes. It's Boxer who's hurt, not me."

She had been waiting for him, listening; perhaps she had heard the police cars. At any rate she had been fearing the worst.

Amanda called, "It's all right, Mrs Gaze. Don't worry. William's all right, it's just Boxer." But she wasn't sure whether she was speaking the truth, because she couldn't see William's wound properly, and it might need stitching or leave a scar.

William's father took Boxer as though he too had

51

been waiting for a catastrophe. "Is he the only one hurt?" he asked.

Amanda nodded.

Mrs Gaze led William into the house, grumbling all the time, saying, "I told you not to go. I knew something terrible would happen. Now you'll be scarred for life. People will think you belonged to a gang. It will be a stigma."

William replied like a small boy, "I want to be scarred. It's an honourable scar," and he tried to laugh.

"Perhaps we should go home," said Marvin.

"I suppose so," agreed Amanda. "Do you think we've done any good?"

"I doubt it," replied Marvin despondently.

"William will never give up now. You know what he thinks of Boxer," said Amanda.

"We can't give in to intimidation," said Marvin.

"Do you think we'll be going out again tonight?"

"I doubt it. The gang will lie low for a bit, after all, the police were pretty near them this time."

"They managed to rob the house, that's the worst of it. I'll go home and ring the others," said Amanda, mounting.

Mr Gaze was washing Boxer down with a bucket of warm water and antiseptic now. He had taken off his coat and rolled up his sleeves. He was very gentle and he talked to Boxer all the time.

"I feel awful," said Amanda, riding away. "Why does everything always happen to the Gazes?"

"It doesn't. *We* were burgled," said Marvin, following her on Skinflint.

Inside the house Mrs Gaze was bathing William's face, while he kept saying, "It's nothing. Can't you leave me alone. I want to look after Boxer."

His eyes kept running because the water stung and he could feel his face swelling and stiffening and one of his legs had started to ache. His father came in slowly and went to the telephone without a word. He was very calm, for he was used to accidents and knew that what was done was done.

William could hear him saying, "It will need stitching. It's pretty bad, I don't know how bad; the muscle could be severed, I don't know. Yes, I shall be here. Fifteen minutes then. Thanks a million, John.

"You've really messed him up this time, William," he said, leaving the telephone. "How did it happen?"

"Spikes and bicycle chains," replied William shortly, his whole face aching now.

"Can't you keep out of trouble for five minutes?"

"I do try."

"It doesn't seem like it."

His mother put a dressing on his face. "You don't need a tetanus shot because you had your last one only a few weeks ago, and it's not deep enough for stitching, but it will leave a scar of course," she said.

He went out to the stable and found Boxer. His wound was still weeping and he was resting his foreleg. He put his arm round his neck and said, "I'm sorry. It must hurt. I didn't mean it to happen." He wished the vet would come with a pain-killer because he could see nothing but pain in Boxer's eyes. He fetched more straw and bedded his loose box deeper than ever and fetched some feed which Boxer wouldn't eat. He remembered all the times they had shared together, good and bad, and he felt like breaking down and weeping into Boxer's damp grey mane.

His mother handed him a mug of tea and said, "Don't grieve, William. I expect he'll be all right."

"He'll be scarred too," William said. "And much worse than me."

"We all have scars," replied his mother.

Now at last the vet was there with pain-killers and needles and thread. He was tall and bare-headed, wearing a water-proof jacket, corduroy trousers, and boots. He looked at Boxer's wound and whistled. "Motor smash up?" he asked.

"No, spikes and bicycle chains," replied William.

"He's been fighting again," said his mother, as though William was a little boy always looking for a scrap.

"For the good of the community," added Mr Gaze.

"Oh, the Pony Patrol again," said the vet, injecting a painkiller into Boxer's neck.

They all knew the routine. They were used to animals being stitched up. They knew what to hand when, and to keep their mouths shut while the vet worked.

"Cup of tea?" asked Mrs Gaze when he had finished.

"Wouldn't mind one." They went inside except for William who stayed behind with Boxer, trying to persuade him to eat and drink.

"I think you had better retire after this," he said finally, before following the others indoors.

The vet was leaving, saying, "I can't tell you anything at this stage. I'll be back tomorrow about lunch time. Don't worry if he doesn't want a lot to eat, he'll be pretty drowsy for the next twenty-four hours."

"Will he ever be sound again?" asked William.

"I can't say yet, it depends how it heals; it's very deep," said the vet.

William sat down and remembered that the patrol was scheduled to ride out again this evening. It was six-thirty now and he felt completely limp. He started to stand up and his mother, who could always read his thoughts, said, "You're not going out again – only over my dead body."

He said, "The Patrol must go on. We have a lot to do."

But she locked the back door and stood barring his way. "If they must go out, let them go alone, without you, William Gaze," she said. "Let *them* get hurt for a change."

He asked, "What do you mean?"

The telephone rang. "You answer," said his mother, still guarding the door.

Both his legs felt stiff as he crossed the hall.

"William Gaze here," he said.

"It's Amanda. I've called off this evening. I've phoned everyone. How's Boxer?" she asked.

"Bad, but did you have to call it off?" he asked.

"Of course. They won't be about tonight. After all, the police were pretty hot on their tails. We are all sure they'll be lying quiet for a couple of days now. How is your face?"

"It's nothing." He was suddenly tired, tired beyond words. He had been steeling himself to go out again, now he could have a hot bath and go to bed.

"I'll be in touch then," he said and hung up.

"It's off. We're not riding tonight," he said, sitting down at the kitchen table, waiting for supper, which he could smell cooking on the stove.

Chapter Six

A tin box

They stayed at home the next day. William nursed Boxer. Alison helped her mother spring-clean. Michael schooled his jumpers. Marvin stayed in bed till noon, much to his mother's annoyance. And Amanda washed Tango's tail and hosed her loose box down with disinfectant and cleaned her tack properly for the first time in weeks. As for Natasha, she left Checked Princess to the gardener's care and caught the train to London and bought herself a handbag for twenty pounds, a mass of make up, and a silk shirt for forty pounds ninety-nine. She lunched with a school friend and returned home at six p.m. All the time it was as though a dark cloud hung over them, promising a deluge of pain and grief in the near future.

William spent the afternoon inspecting all the horses on the farm. Soon some of them would have to go. Several of the ones rescued from the marshes had prospective homes already arranged. The Clydesdale was going to work on the farm as soon as they had found a suitable cart and harness, grey Mermaid was being kept for himself, the foal was to remain until he was older. The local branch of Riding for the Disabled were taking two as soon as the holidays were over, which left only the high-stepping piebald Messenger still seeking a home. He was not easy to place, because some days he wouldn't be caught and he was keen, inclined to shy, and grew impatient waiting at gates. But today William caught them all without trouble and picked out their hoofs and ran his hands over them. "I'll be riding you from now on," he told grey Mermaid, who seemed to have grown a few centimetres as well as filling out in the last few weeks. "You'll have to replace Boxer."

She had a beautiful head now and large eyes which constantly gazed into the distance, and short slim tendons and neat round hoofs.

She didn't want to leave the others but in the end she followed him, stopping at intervals to look back regretfully. He put her into a box next to Boxer where she neighed and rushed round and round, while he thought, she's not really my kind of horse; I like them solid and down to earth and she's frilly and marish, but she will have to do. Outside the sun was shining and the sky was full of dancing clouds. Boxer stood resting his injured foreleg, looking old and sad.

He went indoors and looked at the Heron's Nest and saw that the occupants had come back and were going through the house with two policemen, no doubt counting their losses. He wondered how far they had come and how they felt now, let down by the Pony Patrol and the police. Then his mother called to him, "Letter, William," and he saw the post office van driving away down the drive.

Who can have written? he thought, stumbling

down the stairs two at a time. He thought he recognized the writing – it was squiggly and hardly legible and the address was written too high on the envelope so that the stamp had been stuck at the bottom. It was rather a dirty envelope and, as he looked at it, he was furious to feel his heart pounding against his ribs and his right hand started to shake a little.

His mother stood over him, saying, "What is it, William?" and he said, "Nothing, nothing important," and went into the hall and opened it standing by the telephone.

The writing was on lined paper and there wasn't a date or address, just, *Keep away or you will have it worse the next time. And you won't get better neither.* Signed THE GANG.

His brain said, "Two negatives make a positive," but his hand went on shaking. Then he picked up the telephone and dialled Amanda's number.

"A threatening letter," he said. "We had better ride tonight, just to show them. Otherwise they'll think we're cowards."

"This is Amanda's mother. I don't want you riding tonight, dear. I'm ever so sorry, but I can't have Amanda hurt," said the voice at the other end and rung off.

"Is it bad news?" called his mother from the kitchen.

"Not really," he answered, dialling Alison's number, thinking of old Boxer still between life and death in the stable.

Alison answered, pleased to escape from wiping lampshades with a damp cloth.

"Is that Alison? I've had a threatening letter. I want to ride tonight, just to show them," he said.

58

"I thought the horses were resting," replied Alison.

"We'll have to skip that," he said. "Six o'clock at my place. Okay?"

"Okay," she replied doubtfully.

He telephoned the others one by one. Marvin promised to call on Amanda and talk her into coming. "I can manage her mum, don't worry," he said. "I know how you feel about Boxer. I want my revenge too and the sooner we finish off the gang the sooner we will be able to relax."

Michael said, "I'm delighted. I'm sick of hanging round the garage. I'll be there. How dare they send threatening letters?"

William left a message for Natasha with Nanny who said, "I don't know when she'll be back, but I'll pass it on."

"Tell her to come if she can then," replied William.

"You'll have to give us a contribution to the telephone bill," said Mr Gaze, coming through the hall. "You seem to spend your life hanging on to it."

"Only for another day or two, I hope," replied William.

He ran down to the stable to give Mermaid a feed. He had only ridden her a few times and he knew her back would be up and that she was afraid of high lorries. He felt on edge now, as though they were reaching the end of a road and faced a precipice.

His mother had baked a fruit cake for tea. He ate some listening for the sound of hoofs coming along the drive. He tacked up Mermaid in an eggbutt snaffle and a general purpose saddle. She was sweating already, somehow sensing that excitement lay ahead.

Amanda arrived first on a sweating Tango. "I had a frightful row with Mum," she said.

"I thought Marvin was going to talk her round," replied William.

"Well he didn't succeed."

The air was humid now. Nothing seemed to be moving. There's going to be a thunderstorm, thought William. A minute later Marvin arrived.

"I told Mum I was just going for a hack. I can't stay out too long," he said.

They could hear hoofs clip-clopping along the road now and presently Michael arrived on Bouncer, closely followed by Alison on Rainbow.

They had put on mackintoshes; they all expected a storm.

"Mum's furious," said Alison. "She's gone berserk. I shall probably be locked out when I return home."

"Parents are impossible," replied Marvin. "My mother just shouts and Dad does nothing."

"I'm never going to be a parent," said Amanda.

William led out Mermaid and mounted; her back was up and and she jingled her bit nervously between her teeth and threw her head up and down.

"She's doesn't look very safe," said Marvin.

"She'll have to be," replied William.

"How's Boxer?" asked someone.

"Awful."

"Where are we going?"

"I don't know. I just think we should show ourselves. Anyone want to read the letter?" asked William.

They passed it round. "You should have shown it to the police," said Marvin.

"Where's Natasha?" asked Alison.

"Probably still in London," said William.

"It's the sort of letter you would expect from *them*," said Amanda.

"It's still frightening," replied Alison.

"Let's ride past the Heron's Nest then round all the empty houses – just make it a normal patrol," suggested Amanda.

"Right you are," replied William.

Mermaid was afraid of the other horses, and she wouldn't go first. William missed Boxer who was sensible, down to earth and a hundred per cent reliable. He wondered if he would ever ride him again, and every minute he felt more bitter. Amanda and Alison talked, Marvin and Michael discussed the Pony Club and William felt alone and old, as though he had grown out of the others quite suddenly like you grow out of clothes. All the time the air grew heavier and the clouds drifted lower in the sky.

We need the rain, but not tonight, thought William, when we are riding forth to avenge ourselves. His ears were on the alert. He heard every cracking twig, every slamming door; each car engine sounded different from another as though his ears had been cleaned out and newly trained to separate sounds from one another.

Mermaid danced and pranced and shied at every scrap of paper. Bouncer wouldn't walk. They were all too hot in their mackintoshes. Heron's Nest was locked up and deserted. William looked at it and shouted, "We failed here, didn't we? It was on our list and we failed." Alison thought, he's going mad.

61

Marvin said, "It's the last battle which counts."

"We've got to survive till then. What if it's Skinflint who is cut up next time, and then Rainbow, and Tango and so on? Have you thought of that?" asked William.

"Calm down, William," Alison said. "Shouting doesn't help."

He knew he was near to breaking point and the approaching storm made him worse. He jerked Mermaid in the mouth and she threw up her head and banged him on the nose and he swore, using words he had never uttered before.

"It's all right for you," he cried. "You're not top of the list. It's me they're after."

Then the storm broke, the rain came down in torrents and they started to gallop along the verge looking for shelter.

"Don't stand under a tree," cried Amanda. "Or we'll get struck for certain."

"There must be a shed somewhere," shouted Marvin.

"There's a barn over there," shouted William. "Come on."

They had to cross two fields to reach it. They jumped a hedge followed by a post and rails, while lightning lit the sky in great jagged flashes and thunder crashed simultaneously just above their heads. The horses galloped madly towards the barn, suddenly becoming unstoppable and Amanda screamed above the thunder, "We're going to be struck."

Then they were inside the barn, which was old and thatched and falling down, watching the storm outside, their horses dripping water on to an old stone floor. "It's going to last some time. We might as well dismount," said William.

"Our parents will be in a terrible state," said Amanda.

"Didn't they all jump beautifully," exclaimed Alison.

"My mum only bothers about Skinflint," grumbled Marvin. "She'll dry him off for hours, while she shouts at me for letting him get wet."

"My mother will be feeling sick with anxiety," said Amanda. "She seems to think I'm still about nine years old."

"Mine will be getting a migraine," said Marvin.

Mine will be looking out for me, thought William, worrying without speaking, making me feel guilty.

The barn was almost empty. There were a few old bottles, some fairly new sweet papers, a few bales of rotting straw and an old tin box. William looked at the box for a long time without really seeing it. Then he realized that it didn't fit in with the rest of the barn. Farmers don't leave tin boxes in barns, he thought.

"Hang on to Mermaid someone," he said.

"You're not going out in this, are you?" asked Alison.

"No." He bent down and levered open the lid of the box and looked inside, and suddenly his heart gave a great leap and he shouted, "Come and look. It's full of silver. It's stolen goods. We've found their hideout."

His head started to spin and he pulled out three silver snuff boxes and a great handful of jewellery and Marvin yelled, "That's ours," while Alison shouted, "Don't leave the horses."

It was almost impossible to believe. "Thank God

for the storm," cried Amanda.

"What luck!" cried Alison.

"Won't Mum be pleased!" said Marvin.

"We're not failing any more. We're winning," said Michael.

While Amanda screamed, "Touch wood."

Alison leaned forward and kissed William, which she had been wanting to do for weeks. "Well done again," she said. "Congratulations."

"I thought it looked wrong somehow," he replied, looking embarrassed.

"They'll hate us now," said Michael, still happy.

"And take revenge," replied William, suddenly sober.

"Let's take it to the police because they may be watching us," said Amanda.

"When the thunder has stopped, we had better telephone them. We can dial 999," suggested Michael. "On second thoughts I'll go now. I'm not scared. We can't possibly carry it. Guard it with your lives." He vaulted on to Bouncer and was gone, taking the hedge and the rails in his stride, the rain in his face, the thunder crashing in his ears, the lightning lighting his path.

"He's brave," said Amanda.

"Supposing he gets struck?" said Alison.

"Do stirrups attract lightning?" asked Amanda.

"Shut up, for goodness sake," said Marvin. "He's got rubber treads on his stirrups and rubber boots on his feet and legs, and rubber on his reins. He'll be all right."

"They'll hate us even more after this," said William, staring at the falling rain.

"The box may give a clue. They may be arrested by evening. Then we'll have won," said Marvin, with a note of triumph in his voice.

"I hope they will go to prison for years and years," said Amanda.

Mermaid squealed and kicked at Skinflint who leapt sideways, treading on Marvin's toe. William steadied Mermaid. Marvin held his toe. Outside the sky was growing lighter and the grass smelt wet and new.

"Here he comes," cried Marvin, still holding his toe and hopping up and down.

Michael jumped the hedge and the flight of rails again, Bouncer going calmly and sensibly, with never a falter.

"They are on their way," he said, dismounting. "I explained the situation."

"Did you see the gang or motorbikes?" asked Alison.

"No, nothing. They needn't know we found the stuff," replied Michael.

"They'll see the hoof marks and Rainbow has just peed for the second time," said Alison. "I'm so afraid they will attack William again."

"I shall stay up all night watching for them," replied William.

"I'm going to ask the police for special protection for you. Show them the letter and they will understand," said Amanda.

"All right," he said, taking the creased piece of paper from his pocket.

"They're coming. Look over there – a police car," cried Marvin.

There was a rainbow in the sky and the rumbles of thunder had grown distant and Marvin started to jump up and down, crying, "We're winning. Soon it will be over and we can relax again."

William touched wood slowly and carefully, thinking of Boxer.

"Nothing is over until they are locked up," he said. "This is just the beginning."

But the others were singing now. They sang *You'll Never Walk Alone*. They rushed out to meet the police shouting, "We've found the stolen goods." And suddenly the sky was full of sunlight again and the air full of hope.

Chapter Seven

In search of horses

The police looked stern and solid. They said, "Well done, this *is* a find." William showed them the letter and the tallest one said, "You had better lie low for the time being. They mean what they say."

"Will you keep an eye on his place, officer, please?" asked Amanda, pointing at William.

"We told you to keep out of it, didn't we?" said the other policeman who had ginger hair, a snub nose and freckles.

"But look what we've found," answered Amanda.

"We'll do our best, but we can't make any promises. If we can we will. How's that?" asked the tall one.

"Better than nothing," said Marvin.

They gave William a piece of paper to sign acknowledging that he had handed a chest full of valuables to the police.

They put on gloves to carry the chest away, while the Patrol mounted, pulling up girths and talking to their horses.

"They could have been more grateful," Alison said when the policemen had gone.

67

"They're jealous," replied Amanda. "They should have found it and they didn't."

"Perhaps the insurance company will give us a reward. They were going to advertise for Mum's jewellery in the daily papers," said Marvin.

"I don't care about money. I just want them caught," replied William. Mermaid was cantering sideways now. She didn't obey any leg aids; her nose was in the air and her hocks trailing, instead of being under her.

"I could do with money. I want a new tape recorder," said Marvin.

"And I want a black coat for showing," said Alison.

"And I want a new head collar for Tango. I can't bear her tatty halter a minute longer," cried Amanda.

"And I need twenty pounds' worth of spare parts for my scooter," said Michael.

The sky was clear now, the hawthorn breaking into bud.

"I still can't believe we found it," said Amanda.

The Heron's Nest was deserted, the drawn curtains making it look bereaved.

"We certainly showed ourselves this evening," said Michael. "What will they do when they find their goods gone?"

"Murder me," replied William. "But perhaps they know already. Perhaps they saw the police car. Come on, let's hurry."

The others were singing again now, while he was filled with a sense of dread. They galloped along a grass verge, clattered over a bridge. Then they met a high removal van, which made Mermaid swing round and flee back up the road, nearly unseating

William. He turned her round while the driver of the van switched off his engine. William rode past calling, "Thank you," and he could see that the sun was going down now in the west and another day was almost over.

"I shall feel quite peculiar when it's over," said Amanda. "There will be nothing to think about any more."

William could see the farm now. The cows were back in their meadows. Pete had gone. It must be supper time.

"When they're caught, you mean?" asked Alison.

Amanda nodded.

"They could be caught tonight," said Marvin, laughing.

"The police may be rounding them up at this very minute," cried Alison.

"I hope they get a long prison sentence," cried Michael.

"They need to be taught a lesson," cried Marvin. "They ought to pay for the harm they've done."

The yard was shadowy in the twilight. William sensed that something was wrong. The dogs looked at him with worried eyes; some calves stood huddled together in their pen. Everything was too quiet.

Boxer was lying down. William gave Mermaid's reins to Amanda and knelt down beside him. He wasn't dead, but he had a new gash across his quarters. It looked as though someone had tried to cut a letter on them and failed. William suddenly felt very sick. Boxer was still alive, but only just. He looked mentally shocked, as though he had no wish to go on living. Suddenly William was crying.

"What is it?" asked Amanda, looking at him. "Don't, William. Don't."

"They've been here. Mum and Dad must have been out."

He looked at the dogs and Sadie had a swollen jaw and a half-shut eye. He went across to the calves and saw a tin lying by their pen. It had *Arsenic* written on it. They were all right, just scared. He knew if they had drunk arsenic in their water they would be dead by now.

"They've just been and gone," said William in a voice without any expression. "They must have seen us in the barn."

He looked at the calves' water and started to bale it out with a bucket. Michael helped. Suddenly no one wanted to talk any more. William saw that the car was missing. Where were his parents? Supposing they've killed them, he thought, lured them to their death. For the first time in his life he wished he was dead, at peace somewhere under the earth, then he was overcome with rage.

"When I meet them I'll pull them to pieces," he cried. "I'll fight them with anything I can find. And if I kill them I'll be pleased."

"Do you think any of the calves have drunk the water?" asked Amanda, looking at the trough.

"No, they were too scared. Wait a sec, while I go inside."

The kettle had boiled dry on the Aga. The table was laid ready for supper. William looked around for clues, but there were none.

He went outside. "My parents have been lured away," he said.

"We had better go through the house," said Michael, after a moment's stunned silence. "You needn't come if you don't want to."

William knew what he was thinking – that they

71

might be somewhere inside, which meant the gang had taken the car.

"I'll come," he said.

Alison was weeping. "Why does it always happen to him?" she moaned. "It isn't fair."

Marvin was tying up the horses. Dusk had come suddenly.

There was one word written across the sitting-room wall – PIGS. Some of the furniture had been smeared with cow dung. His mother's best china had been taken out of a cabinet and smashed; that was all. There was no sign of his parents.

"They always leave a message if they go out unexpectedly," he said.

"On this occasion there wasn't time. Don't despair, mate. We'll win," said Michael, putting a hand on his shoulder.

"I've never hated anyone as much as I hate them," said William.

"Can I telephone my mother?" asked Amanda.

"Help yourself," replied William.

"I think we'll have to call the police," said Michael.

He had taken charge now. William was too stunned and bewildered to think coherently any more. He kept imagining his mother locked up somewhere, and when he looked at the dogs' reproachful eyes he knew it was all his fault.

Alison was mixing Boxer a feed. Marvin was watering the horses from a bucket. Then Michael shouted, "Come here. I've found something," and waved an envelope with squiggly writing on it, right at the top where the stamp should be.

"Open it! Hurry up!" yelled William in a tortured voice.

"It's addressed to you."

"Open it."

"Where was it?" shouted Alison.

"In the front door knocker."

"I know the writing," said William.

"It says, it says . . . Oh help," cried Michael.

"Read it!" screamed William.

"It says,

*'You asked for it, and you've got it. No one plays about
with us. Your horses are on the motorway – or they were,
they're most likely in little bits by now. Got it, chum?
You were warned, The Gang.'* "

'Nothing about my parents. We had better ring
the police," said William.

He walked indoors like a sleepwalker, while
Michael was already dialling 999, saying, "Have
there been any accidents on the motorway? Any
loose horses. No, nothing. I want to report a
missing car too – what's the number?"

Alison was weeping again, saying, "Poor
William, poor Boxer," while he felt stunned, as
though he was sleepwalking, as though everything
was happening to someone else, not to William
Gaze at all.

It was evening now.

"The police say the motorway is clear, there's
been no reports of loose horses," said Michael,
putting down the telephone receiver. "They
haven't seen your car either. Do you think your
parents could be looking for the horses? They
could have found the note and put it back."

"Impossible," replied William. "A, because they
would have left a message if it had only been
horses, B, because this place must have been empty
when the gang came; the dogs would have alerted

73

my parents at once otherwise."

"They must be looking for you then."

"Yes. That's why they didn't leave a message," said William.

"So they may come back all right?" asked Alison, still sobbing.

"It's possible," replied Michael.

"What are we going to do then?" asked Amanda.

"They probably received a telephone call," suggested Alison.

"We had better tour the farm looking for clues, then start looking for the horses. I've got a bike with lights, and so has Mum, and there's an old one of Pete's with tyres which need pumping up," William said.

"I'll go home and get mine," said Amanda.

"So will I. Back in five minutes," cried Marvin. "I'll telephone Natasha too. We need lots of people."

Alison and Michael put their horses in the stable and telephoned their parents. William looked at Boxer's wound again and decided to leave it for the time being. He was horribly afraid that Boxer was going to die. He seemed listless and without any will to survive, as though he had had enough and had lost all faith in humans, and this made William angry and sadder than ever. He sat by Boxer saying, "It wasn't meant to happen; all humans are not like this," and the old horse slowly rubbed his head against William's arm. But the feed Amanda had mixed for him stayed uneaten and he wasn't thirsty either. William had seen animals before which had stopped wanting to live in the same way – terrified baby rabbits, wounded birds, sick cows who had lost their calves. This is the worst day of my life, decided William, standing up at last, and I've seen some pretty awful ones in my time.

Meanwhile Amanda was home, shouting at her mother, "I've got to go whatever you say. My bike has got a light."

"Why can't the police deal with it?"

"I've got to go, that's all I know," cried Amanda, shouting and crying at the same time.

"But it's dark and you've had no supper."

"The horses are lost – Suzy, and all the ones we rescued last year. They'll be killed on the roads, on the motorway. Just imagine it Mum, please."

She was on her bike now, riding away, praying all the time, "God help William. Please God help us find the horses and William's parents safe and sound. Please God I will believe in you for ever if you just grant it for me, please." She fell into the drive hedge because automatically she had shut her eyes; but she wasn't hurt. She kept imagining a great pile up on the motorway with Marmaduke, Misty, Suzy and the others in the middle of it. Lights flashing, the wail of police sirens and ambulances, the awful horror of it all. She remounted her bicycle which was too small and which she had named Black Beauty years ago when she was nine and, keeping her eyes open, she continued to pray, "God help William."

Marvin was trying to keep calm. "You are over protective," he told his mother firmly. "I'm old enough now to go out at nine in the evening to avoid a major catastrophe, so please stop nagging."

His head was aching and he could feel his asthma coming on.

"Skinflint is really Skinflint now," complained his mother. "He's all run up and his legs are filled. You're not fit to have a decent pony."

"We found all your jewellery in a barn today, you're getting it back," said Marvin. "Aren't you grateful?"

"But how?" she asked, her voice changing.

"It's a long story," replied Marvin, suddenly feeling at least eighteen years old. "I'll tell you when I get back."

"Tell me now. Did you say *all* . . .?"

"I think so. The police have got it. Ring them up," said Marvin, pedalling away in the dusk.

He loved the twilight. Suddenly his asthma was gone. Soon there will be a moon, he thought.

"What am I to tell your father? He'll be back from the pub in a moment," called his mother.

"Anything. I don't care," shouted Marvin.

Alison, William and Michael were waiting now, biting their nails, halters and head collars wound round their waists, their pockets bulging with oats.

"Let's meet them by the end of the drive, come on," said Michael.

William felt drugged with misery, he kept seeing Boxer helpless in his box, the dogs' accusing eyes, the empty house and he knew it was all his fault. He had been blind and stupid when he should have given up. He had been warned by the police, warned by his parents; he had ignored them all. Now, if the horses were in the middle of a pile up on the motorway, it was his fault and if his parents never came back it was his fault too, and it was almost more than he could bear. If that happens, I shall kill myself, he thought. Finish myself off.

"Come on," called Michael. "Aren't you coming? The others are here. Wake up."

"I think he should stay behind. I do really," said Alison suddenly. "If he stayed at home he could wait for his parents, and explain everything."

"I've left a note for them saying *Gone in search of horses*," said William. "I'm not staying." He thought, that would be worse than anything, sitting and waiting, letting the minutes tick away, doing nothing.

Chapter Eight

On the motorway

"We're not a pony patrol, we're a bicycle patrol," said Amanda, trying to cheer the others up. But no one answered. The moon was rising now, lighting up mad, scurrying clouds, making everything mysterious, magical. Then Natasha appeared riding Checked Princess and wearing a fluorescent waistcoat and a light on her stirrup.

"No one told me you were going to be on bikes," she said.

"It doesn't matter," replied William.

"Where are you going?" asked Natasha, doing an extended trot along the road.

"To the motorway," replied Michael.

They didn't want to talk, because suddenly everything was too bad for words.

"But that's several kilometres away," cried Natasha.

"Only ten or eleven and we may find them on the way," retorted Michael, standing on the pedals of his bike.

There was a grass verge now. Michael had Pete's bike and streaked ahead. Checked Princess galloped on the grass. Alison struggled on Mrs

Gaze's old-fashioned bike and kept calling, "Wait for me," though Amanda was only just ahead on Black Beauty. Somewhere in the middle pedalled William, head down, not speaking to anyone.

"Eleven kilometres," he thought, "ten, nine, eight, seven . . . How long will it take us? If only we were old enough to drive."

And then, at last, they could see the distant lights of the motorway, like a path through the night, lit up by fairy lights. The cars moved quickly like lit-up insects in the distance, headlights instead of eyes.

"The traffic is still moving, so there's still hope," shouted Michael over his shoulder, slowing down a little.

"It may not be moving in both lanes," answered William.

The land was flat, the horizon criss-crossed by motorway bridges. Their legs ached.

"Let's look as we go. There may be hoof marks. How could they be so sure they were on the motorway anyway?" asked Amanda.

"They could have driven them here on their bikes," shouted Michael.

"Or along the old railway track," cried William. "Then no one would have seen them. It comes out near the motorway, where it used to join the main line to London. Remember?"

"Yes," cried Michael, sounding desperate.

Soon they started to flag down cars, crying, "Have you seen a bunch of horses?"

Some cars wouldn't stop. Some drivers were rude; others said things like, "Have you told the police?" or "I'll keep my eyes open. Who can I contact if I find them?"

"They may still be on the old railway track," cried Michael.

"I hope they are," cried Amanda.

"Wouldn't it be lovely. We could drive them home and then, if your parents were home, William, the nightmare would be over," said Alison.

"It won't be over until the gang is locked up, not as far as I'm concerned anyway," said William.

"Dad's got guards with dogs patrolling our place. It's fantastic," exclaimed Natasha.

They were only three kilometres from the motorway now and it didn't look like a model any more, but real. And then suddenly there was a terrific bang, which sent Checked Princess leaping into the ditch and made Alison fall off her bicycle screaming, "What was that?"

"It came from the motorway," shouted Michael.

"No, I can't bear it!" shrieked Amanda.

And now none of them had ever bicycled so fast before. Natasha let Checked Princess gallop flat out along the road, ignoring the damage it would do to her legs. William put all his strength into his legs. Amanda cursed Black Beauty for being so small, and cursed her parents for refusing to buy her a bigger bike. None of them knew what they expected to find.

Then the sirens started. First police cars flashed by, next a fire engine, then ambulances. They lost count of them. And they could see the roundabout now, the motorway signs, and everything was suddenly quiet, too quiet.

"I'm afraid to go on. I don't want to see it," said Amanda.

"See what?" asked Michael.

"I don't know."

"Bikes aren't allowed on the motorway," said Marvin. "Anyway, it's too late; either the horses are on the motorway cut to pieces, or they're not. It's as simple as that."

"Nothing is that simple," argued William.

"I don't want to go on either. I can't bear tragedy. I'm like Mum. We're not made for it," said Natasha.

"Horses aren't allowed on the motorway either," observed Marvin.

"Except by mistake," muttered William.

And all the time they were still moving, slower than before, but still forward towards the motorway.

When they reached the roundabout, they threw down their bikes.

"I'll stay with Natasha and Checked Princess if you don't mind. I can't stand any more disaster," said Amanda.

"We'll walk along the hard shoulder," said Michael, ignoring her.

They could see a pile-up in the distance, black smoke, a lorry on fire.

"If the horses are mixed up in that, we won't see them again – ever," said Michael.

"They could be grazing on the bank," suggested Alison.

"Terribly injured of course," said Marvin, trying to sound matter-of-fact.

"Yes, terribly injured," agreed William.

Two ambulances flashed by in the opposite lane, their sirens wailing. Black smoke belched steadily into the night sky.

"It must be a petrol lorry," said Michael.

"There's a stench of rubber too," said Marvin.

They were talking without really listening or thinking, just to stay sane.

"Do you believe in horoscopes?" asked Alison. "Mine said, *don't travel in the middle of the month*. And I am, aren't I?"

"It was nice of Natasha to come, but she's not much use," said Marvin.

"Here come the police," said William, stopping in his tracks.

"What do you want?" called a policeman wearing an orange fluorescent jacket.

"Are there any horses mixed up in the crash?" cried Michael, because suddenly William couldn't speak.

"Horses?" cried the policeman. "Now why should there be horses?"

He's Irish, thought William without the thought really registering because now he was overwhelmed with relief.

"We thought they might have strayed here," said Michael.

"Well they didn't. Now get off home quick. This is no place for kids," replied the policeman.

"Thank you, thank you very much," cried William.

"Don't mention it," answered the policeman, going back to the *Police Accident* signs and the horror which lay beyond.

"We had better go back," said Michael.

"It must have been a straightforward crash," said Alison.

"If crashes are ever straightforward," replied Michael. "You should see some of the wrecks Dad gets. It's incredible."

"Where are the horses then?" asked Alison.

They were all feeling weak at the knees with relief and a little light-headed.

"We had better hurry," cried Alison. "Amanda and Natasha are still suffering agonies."

"It seems odd to be walking along an empty motorway in the middle of the night," said Marvin.

"What's the time then?" asked William.

"Nearly midnight."

"I wonder who the gang are burgling now," said Marvin.

"It's a perfect night for them with the police on the motorway and us searching for horses," replied William bitterly.

"I feel as though I will never be afraid of anything again after tonight," said Alison.

"If only the night was over," answered Marvin. "And we had found the horses."

"If only ... the saddest words in the English language," replied William, wondering whether Boxer was still lying down with his sad head buried in the straw.

Amanda was calling now. "Any luck? What's happening?"

"Nothing, the horses aren't there," called Michael.

"I think we had better go home and wait for another day," said Marvin. "They may be miles away by now."

"I didn't tell anyone where I was going. If Dad comes home I'm for it. He doesn't trust me an inch since my brother went to pieces," said Natasha, mounting Checked Princess.

"We're all going to be in trouble and we haven't achieved anything," replied Amanda, astride Black Beauty, thinking of her parents sitting up for her at home growing angrier and angrier.

"Dad will understand," said Michael.

"Mine won't," replied Marvin. "Not in a month of Sundays. He'll be in a red hot mood."

"My parents . . ." began William and then remembered that they were missing. "I want to get home now," he said. "I must. To the devil with the horses."

"It must have been an awful crash," said Amanda, pedalling furiously. "Look, there's still smoke in the sky."

"People are such fools," said Michael.

"Obviously the petrol lorry crashed first and the others went into it," replied Marvin.

"Because people are such fools," repeated Michael.

William wasn't listening, his mind was far away imagining his parents fighting the gang. His father was slow and strong and incredibly heavy; his mother was quick but her arms were like matchsticks. They wouldn't stand a chance against bicycle chains and knives.

"Stop! Look! over there! There's a man waving," cried Amanda after a few minutes.

He was standing down a side road. He was old and red faced with a dog at his heels.

He called, "Are you looking for some horses?"

"Yes, we are," shouted Michael.

"They were heading for the motorway. They came up from the old railway track. They were like mad things, five or six of them, a few hours ago now." He smelt of drink. "Lucky I saw you. I was just taking Sally for a walk last thing, like."

"Where are they now?" said Michael.

"I drove them into a field just yonder. I shut the

84

gate. It runs down to the railway line; there isn't much grass and I don't know how the fence is, but I think they are still there."

They shouted their thanks. "We're achieving something at last," cried Amanda.

"Let's hurry," cried William.

"They *were* heading for the motorway then," said Marvin.

They ran, throwing down their bikes when they reached the field. The grass was wet with dew already. Soon the cocks would herald another day.

"Where are they?" shrieked Alison.

"I don't know and the moonlight will be gone soon," cried Amanda.

"There, look!" cried Natasha, higher than the others on Checked Princess. "Look, they're down on the railway line."

"The real one?" screamed William.

"Yes."

"The London train one?" choked Alison.

But Natasha was galloping now, screaming over her shoulder, "There may be a train coming, run." She could see that the signal was up and that the level crossing gates were shut in the distance. The big Clydesdale had his quarters on the rails as he grazed the bank. Misty, the foal, was wandering beside the rails. The fence between the field and the line lay a tangled heap of wire, surrounded by bits of paper and old bottles. The other horses grazed the banks, oblivious of danger.

"You get the horses, I'll stop the train. There's one about this time. My parents come on it," cried Natasha, looking at the small jewelled watch on her left wrist.

She knew which way the train would come. The

others had already reached the wire. She pushed Checked Princess into a gallop and could hear a distant roar. She started to gallop alongside the train. She had galloped so fast that the train was still a hundred metres away from the horses and now it was stopping. Windows were being flung open. "There are horses on the line," screamed Natasha. "*Horses*. Pull the communication cord."

The others were leading the horses through the gap. A bird was screaming in the sky. "Natasha," cried her mother, "what are you doing?" as the train drew to a groaning grinding halt.

The driver and his guard shouted at William.

"Why don't you look after your b...... horses. There could have been an accident."

William was too weary to reply. It seemed like the final horror on a horrific day. He doubted he would ever find peace again anywhere – but at least the horses were safe.

Michael tried to explain. Natasha told her parents not to worry. "We were looking for the horses. Now we've found them. Everything is going to be all right," she said.

The driver got back into the train, saying that he would be sending a full report to London in the morning. Some drunkards shouted rude remarks at Natasha out of the window.

"Now we can go home," said William. "I want my bed more than anything else on earth," and he wondered whether the house would still be empty when he reached it.

Chapter Nine

"It's them"

"I wish the night was over," said Marvin as the train thundered away.

"It is. Look over there. It's dawn," said Amanda.

"Stupid horses!" cried William, jerking at Marmaduke's head collar rope.

"What are we going to do with our bikes?" asked Alison.

"I'll leave mine and ride Marmaduke," said William. "Leg me up, someone." He always felt better on a horse, braver, less pessimistic. It was as though he belonged there.

Marvin decided to keep his bike. William said he would lead Misty. The east was growing light already.

Amanda vaulted on to bay Maple Leaf who still had a backbone which stood up like a bent bough. Alison climbed on to Suzy from a bank. They decided to lead the others. It was very dark now, except where the sun was rising with all the promise of another fine day.

"We're nearly through," said Michael, pedalling Pete's old bike. "We've beaten them at every turn. We have the stolen goods and the horses. The

88

calves are still alive in spite of arsenic in their water. Now we only have to find Mr and Mrs Gaze."

"Which may be easier said than done," answered Natasha. "And they nearly killed the horses, didn't they? If it hadn't been for that man walking his dog . . .!"

"God is on our side. And we may not have to find the Gazes. They may be at home waiting for William," cried Amanda.

She felt more cheerful now, as though she had got her second wind. She had been exhausted, but she was no longer; quite suddenly she felt as though she could go on for ever.

There were rabbits everywhere, foxes, hedgehogs. At this hour they seemed to own everything. It was as though the countryside had suddenly become theirs and they were free at last to do what they liked without fear of humans and their terrible motor cars. Everything was very quiet – so quiet that you could hear the snuffle of a hedgehog or the breathing of a fox.

"I think I will become nocturnal," said Amanda after a time. "It's so peaceful and happy compared with day-time."

"Touch wood," cried Alison.

The ponies dawdled, full of grass. William was in a hurry, consumed by the thought of his parents injured somewhere, slowly dying. He didn't want to talk, and he had seen too many dawns to be impressed by the silence and the mystery and the night life of animals.

He kicked Marmaduke with his heels and shouted, but the big horse only cocked an ear back and moved on at the same steady lumbering pace knowing nothing of time and ticking clocks, thinking instead of mangers full of oats and chaff, and of standing under a tree when the day grew hot.

The other horses were equally happy, having enjoyed their night out. None of them was in a hurry to get anywhere; they were at peace with the world, their stomachs full, their legs exercised. Only Checked Princess sweated and jogged, wanting to get home among her friends.

Amanda tried to talk to William but he had shut himself off from the world and didn't hear. And slowly dawn came with a great crowing of cocks in the distance and the sound of engines starting.

And then suddenly Alison stopped and said, "Listen! Someone's screaming."

And Marvin answered, "There can't be. I can't hear anything. You're just imagining things."

But they all stopped just the same and for a moment they could hear nothing but the horses' breathing.

Then Alison cried, "It's over there."

And Amanda said, "Down the little lane; there's a post office in the front room of the cottage, a tiny place. You can see the post box. Look!"

"I've been there," replied Marvin. "A sweet old couple keep it."

"There's no sound now," said Natasha.

"Tie up the horses," cried William. "Quickly. I can see a van. Look! It's them!"

And suddenly they were all consumed with a feeling of dread and excitement and fear, all evenly mixed.

"We haven't got any weapons," said Michael, quietly looking round.

"We'll fight with our hands then," answered William.

There were trees and a fence. They tied up the ponies, quickly and firmly, and then they were running silently, without speaking, down a short straight lane and William was thinking, this is it! This is the end. This is where we meet, and his hands were shaking with desire for the fight to begin, for the chance to pay someone back for what had been done to Boxer, for revenge.

Michael was longing for a fight too, for the feel of a fist against fist, and the sheer thrill of struggling, matching strength with strength. Marvin was praying that his asthma wouldn't come on, that he would be able to hold his own and come out intact. Amanda and Alison were hoping for weapons, for handy chairs and walking sticks, even saucepans, while Natasha looked at her nails and was glad that they were long and hard and varnished.

The cottage was small and thatched, with neat lattice windows and honeysuckle growing up the outer walls. There was a notice which read *Stoneyfeld Post Office* and a small red letter box, and a telephone kiosk a few metres away. It was a pretty place which was full of hollyhocks in summer and primroses in spring. Now one of the windows was smashed and the old-fashioned front door was open. A van was parked across the gateway and there were three motorbikes leaning against a hedge. William's heart was thumping against his ribs now and they were all afraid of what was to come.

"They're inside," whispered Michael, while Amanda found a large stone and picked it up, and Marvin rolled up his sleeves automatically, without thinking.

"Ready?" muttered William and rushed inside with Michael close behind. Marvin stopped only to pick up a boot scraper, while Alison grabbed a stand for milk bottles as a suitable weapon.

The small post office seemed full of people; the telephone was lying on the floor, a bottle of sweets lay in smithereens, there were papers scattered everywhere. The counter was smashed. William went straight for a youth in a motorbike helmet, while the others plunged into the next room where an old lady was tied to a chair and a youth was twisting an old man's arm, shouting at the same time, "Where is it? Where's the money? I'll break it then, mate."

Amanda and Alison plunged upstairs where they could hear booted feet trampling while Michael and Marvin went for the youth. Marvin used a rugger tackle which sent him on to his knees, while Natasha ran to the kiosk outside to call the police. William was getting the worst of his fight in the front room which was the post office proper. His head was battered and bleeding, but he was beyond feeling pain. He was avenging Boxer's hurt, and nothing hurt as much as that hurt. He knew his shirt was ripped to shreds, but he was still hanging on. If the crash helmet hadn't been there, he could have won. His head was spinning now, but he kept it down while he forced the youth inch by inch backwards across the room, away from the door, away from escape and retreat until someone else came to help him. He was like a terrier holding on to a rat. Nothing but death or unconsciousness was going to make him let go.

Marvin was undoing the cord which bound the

old woman now, comforting her. The old man was stumbling towards the stairs, while Michael called, "Hold it, Grandpa," as he bound up the youth.

Then Amanda came head first down the stairs screaming, "My mouth, my mouth. I've broken a tooth," and suddenly Michael and Marvin were leaping the cottage stairs three at a time, with the old man close behind brandishing a walking stick.

Alison was on the floor on her face with two youths laughing at her, but not for long. Marvin had never fought before as he was fighting now, and Michael rushed in with a judo tackle which sent one of them straight over his shoulder, crashing into the wall. There were bits of mattress everywhere and the familiar PIGS painted across the wallpaper in red. The youths were putting up a terrific fight, but now in the distance they could all hear the wail of sirens.

Downstairs, Natasha was helping William while the old lady watched. There was blood on the floor but the youth was down now. Natasha sat on his shoulders while the old lady found some post office string to bind his legs. And then suddenly everything was quiet, which meant that the battle was over, that the Patrol had won. The old man was trembling uncontrollably now, but he was alert and still alive to what was happening.

William wiped the blood from his mouth and Natasha said, "You can have your tooth crowned, Amanda. Don't worry. Honestly, I promise." Her red hair had come down and lay around her face. Her hands were spattered with William's blood. But they had won and for a moment that was all that mattered.

Upstairs, the old man put a cushion under

Alison's head and she muttered, "I'm all right, quite all right. Have they gone?"

And Michael, looking at the youths lying on the small bedroom floor, squirming feebly, said, "No, we've beaten them."

And Marvin said, "A thousand times over."

Downstairs, the old lady found Amanda some paper handkerchiefs. And put a towel round William's head, murmuring, "Poor young fellow."

And now car lights were lighting the cottage and heavy feet trod the garden path.

William looked at the policemen and said, "They're here, and upstairs. You may have to carry them down," and he tried to smile and one of them said, "You look as though you need carrying yourself."

The cottage rooms had been built hundreds of years ago when people were smaller. The policemen had to bend their heads and now there was hardly room to move, so William stepped outside into the morning air and saw that day had really arrived.

He sat on a bank and his head spun and he felt very weak and rather strange. A policeman telephoned for ambulances while two others handcuffed the youths and dragged them towards the police cars. And William thought how small and mean they looked now that they were beaten. Then Amanda sat down beside him and said, "I feel all weak at the knees. Do you think we can ride home?"

And William answered, "Of course. Why not? I'm just waiting for the police to go."

"Do I look awful?" Amanda asked next. "Look at me."

94

Her face was bloodstained, her mouth swollen, and her eyes heavy with lack of sleep with a great bruise below one which was slowly swelling.

"Not awful. You never look awful," said William, trying to be gallant. "You just look as though you've taken a beating, that's all."

"Thank you very much," replied Amanda, trying to smile, but wincing instead.

"Here come the ambulances," said Natasha. "I'm all right. How about you?"

"We're all right," replied Amanda.

The ambulance men carried the old couple outside first, calling them "Gran and Grandad".

Then they brought out Alison, protesting loudly, on a stretcher. "I was only out a minute," she cried. "And Mum will be furious, and what about my horse?"

But they simply ignored her. "We had better slip away before they see us," said William to Amanda. "Come on."

Natasha was talking to Checked Princess who was frightened of the stretchers and Michael and Marvin were making faces at the youths through the windows of the police cars.

"We're going," said William. "Come on." He vaulted on to Marmaduke and then they were moving again through the misty morning air.

"Mission accomplished," announced Michael cheerfully. "I feel fine, thanks to judo."

"I want my bed," said Amanda. "I feel quite sick with exhaustion."

"I want my parents to be safe and sound," said William. "And Boxer to live; that's all that matters now."

Chapter Ten

"The best vet in England"

It was eight kilometres to home, long weary kilometres, but Michael, Natasha, Marvin and Amanda were triumphant. They called it, "the road to victory", and sang songs, loudly and out of tune. They kept saying, "We've won. Cheer up, William. You wanted the gang put away and they are now. It's a hundred per cent victory."

But he couldn't sing, not with Boxer lying half dead in his loose box at home and his parents still missing. He tried, but the words died in his throat.

The roads were full of people racing late to work, they drove round corners like maniacs in brand-new cars, hooting. They nearly ran into the horses and William muttered, "Fools" to himself over and over again as though the words somehow gave him comfort. And the road home was straight and flat with nothing but fields and beautiful trees and verges full of spring flowers. They took it in turns to ride and bicycle, and then at last they saw the farm in the distance and they had come to the parting of the ways. Natasha and Michael said goodbye.

"I'll telephone you as soon as I get home to hear

about your parents and Boxer. You don't mind me going, do you?" Natasha asked. "My parents are sure to be in one hell of a mood."

"Of course not."

"And if you can manage without me, I'll go too," said Michael. "If I can borrow this bike until tomorrow."

"Of course," said William. "It's Pete's, but he won't mind."

Riding on, Amanda said, "I feel faint with hunger. When did we last eat?"

"I can't remember," replied Marvin.

Misty dragged and dawdled whereas Maple Leaf pulled, and Suzy jogged and Marmaduke simply went on plodding, making William think, they are as different as we are!

As they drew near to the farm, his stomach started to flutter and there was a dry feeling in his throat and he started to think, supposing my parents aren't there? What then? To try to imagine life without them. The farm up for sale? The horses going? Where would he go? To Aunt Jennie living in a semi-detached house in Cambridge? Or to Uncle Geoff and Auntie Mary in Wales? Or would he simply leave school as soon as possible and start work? Or take on the farm single handed? He felt muddled and tired, and now he could see everything clearly, the low farm buildings, the old-fashioned three-chimneyed house, the cows waiting to be milked, the great elms which somehow had survived elm disease. And he knew how much he loved the place, that however far he travelled, it would always be home.

And then Amanda started to shout, "Look, the car's there."

And suddenly they were all trotting, with William yelling, "Mum, Dad, are you there?"

Mr and Mrs Gaze came out to meet them, waving and calling, "Well done. The police phoned to say you were on your way."

And they looked tired and fraught, but otherwise normal, so that suddenly William felt in a strange way that he had been let down, and that all the agony had been for nothing.

His mother kissed him and his father slapped him on the back.

"What happened to you? You weren't here. There was no message or anything. We thought you were dead," said William in reproachful tones.

"We were telephoned. A most educated voice informed us that you had fallen off your horse and were walking home from Siddons Farm. They said that you were concussed and had a head injury and wouldn't accept help. They knew your name and everything," related Mrs Gaze.

"But Siddons Farm is twenty-four kilometres away," cried William. "I hardly ever ride that far."

"The message sounded so real, and the voice was so educated," said Mrs Gaze, as though educated people were always to be trusted. "I couldn't help thinking it was true. We looked for you for three blessed hours and when we came back here, we phoned the police."

The others were turning out the horses now.

"You know what happened while you were away?" asked William slowly.

"Not properly," she said.

"You've seen Boxer?"

"Yes," said Mr Gaze. "And I'm afraid there's no

hope for him, William. He's given up the will to live."

"He's not dead, is he?"

"Not yet."

"We've got to get a vet," cried William.

"You know what a vet will say," asked his father.

"Not a good vet; not the best in England," cried William. "And I want the best vet in England. Boxer's worth it. He's mine and I'm not having him destroyed."

"I should have Mr Foxley," said Marvin quietly. "He's the best horse vet there is; he travels with the Olympic team. He's a proper specialist. He lives only eighty kilometres away from here. He'll come at once. He's that sort of person."

"Thank you," said William, walking slowly towards the stable, wanting to make sure that Boxer was alive before he telephoned anybody.

In the house Amanda was telephoning her parents, saying, "Yes, everything is all right. We've caught the gang and found the loot. We've won." Saying such words made her suddenly realize how much they had accomplished and she couldn't keep a note of triumph out of her voice – so much in twenty-four hours, she thought. What an achievement!

Meanwhile, watched by Marvin, William knelt beside Boxer, saying softly, "Come on, Boxer. They're caught. They'll never touch you again."

A feed waited unseen by Boxer's head and water undrunk. The wound on his quarters was newly washed and clean, and the whole loose box smelt of antiseptic. But now there didn't seem much hope. Boxer didn't even move his head, or look at William. He was almost lifeless. William stood up, slowly stretching stiff knees and said in a toneless voice, "I'll go and telephone Mr Foxley. Thanks for everything, Marvin."

"Best of luck," replied Marvin, unable to think of anything else to say.

"What about my bike?" shouted Pete, the farm-hand. "You took it without asking."

"It will come back," shouted William.

Amanda's mother had come now. She looked bright and pretty and made up, as though she belonged to another world. And William saw how dirty and bedraggled he was for the first time, and that his parents looked as though they had slept in their clothes, which no doubt they had. And he wondered how some people managed to survive without catastrophe while others were perpetually struggling for survival.

"Hurry up, Marvin," shouted Amanda. "We're taking you home."

They all wanted to sleep now, but first William had to telephone Mr Foxley. He had to find his telephone number with eyes which would hardly stay open and talk to a receptionist he didn't know. He had to explain that Boxer was dying of shock and try to make them understand that the case was urgent, and it wasn't easy. The receptionist said, "What is the complaint?" and "Are you sure it isn't simply old age. You know old horses do sometimes lie down and never get up again. It's quite common. They simply reach the end and give up just like you describe."

She was very kind and patient, and tried to make William understand that Boxer didn't need Mr Foxley. William felt like weeping with despair.

"He's got this gash on his quarters. It could be

that," he said at last.

"You mean tetanus?"

"Yes," he answered, though he knew it wasn't likely as Boxer had had shots of anti-tetanus vaccine all through his life. But his lie had the right effect.

"Why didn't you say that before?" asked the receptionist. "Mr Foxley will be with you by lunch time."

"Lunch time!" exclaimed William. "What's the time now then?"

"Ten o'clock," she said and rang off.

He ate some cereal with milk and sugar, then fell into a chair and slept, dreaming of a railway line with trains racing towards each other while someone screamed, "Help!" and he yelled, "Stop!" Then as the trains met, each travelling at a hundred and fifty kilometres an hour, he saw that Boxer was between them. He woke with tears running down his face and his mother saying, "What is it, William? Are you all right?"

"Of course," he said. "It was just a dream. How is Boxer? Has the vet been?"

"No. You've only been asleep ten minutes," she answered. "Why don't you go upstairs and lie down properly?"

He shook his head; he had not the energy to move. He felt dopey with exhaustion. He slept again and dreamed that the gang were burning down the farmhouse; he telephoned the fire brigade, but they wouldn't answer, and now he knew that his father was saying, "The vet has come, William," and *that* was reality and the rest a dream.

He looked in a mirror and saw that his hair was matted with blood and his face was smeared with dirt, but compared to Boxer dying it was nothing. He tried to run, but his legs refused to obey his command so he had to walk, slowly and stiffly like an old man.

Mr Foxley was talking to his father when he reached the stable. He was dark haired and tall with long fingers and a straight nose.

He looked at William and said, "We'll put him on a drip. That will feed him for a time and we'll give an injection of vitamin B. We want to keep him going until he recovers from his state of shock."

"Do you think he'll live then?" asked William.

"He's got a fighting chance."

Mr Foxley worked quickly and efficiently, without talking, except for an occasional soothing word to Boxer. When he had attached the tube which supplied the drip, he sat beside Boxer, stroking his neck. "You'll have to stay with him," he told William. "He mustn't get up with the drip like this. If he does, move the bottle and attach it to the side of the box; then keep him tied up so he gets the whole lot. I'll be back this evening about five. Either he'll be better by then, or he'll be dead."

"Thank you for coming."

"He needs quiet. He mustn't be upset, and keep the top door shut for the time being. Okay?"

"Yes."

William sat in the straw beside his shocked horse. Time passed slowly. His mother brought him lunch on a tray and said something about reporters wanting information for the local paper and he said, "Tell them to ring Amanda." Later she said something about television and he said, "Tell them to ring Natasha. She would look wonderful on telly." And all the time, he was watching Boxer, waiting for some movement, something to give him hope.

His father brought him coffee, muttering about television, and he said, "Leave it till tomorrow."

And it was two o'clock now and Boxer hadn't moved or stirred. William lay in the straw and thought about life, how nothing was ever fair, and he knew it was nearly three o'clock by the sounds outside, and he started to give up hope. He wondered if the gang were sorry for what they had done, and how they were being treated by the police and what had brought them to such cruelty. And he wondered whether they would ever change, and slowly Boxer stirred and moved his eyes and looked at him. William stroked Boxer's cheek and took an ear and whispered into it, "Boxer, get well. It's over and done with. There's nothing ahead for you but peace," and he hoped it was true.

Next Boxer stretched his legs each in turn, as though he were testing them and then he looked at William as though trying to say, "Why are you here?"

"I'm watching the drip," William said.

Boxer was breathing more loudly now, and, looking up at the bottle from which the drip was coming, William saw that three quarters of the liquid inside had gone. He took hold of the container and waited, knowing that somehow he must ensure the drip continued to function whatever happened. Boxer rolled over a little and stretched his forelegs in front of him.

He shook his old grey head a little while William waited.

He moved his hindlegs under him, while William

104

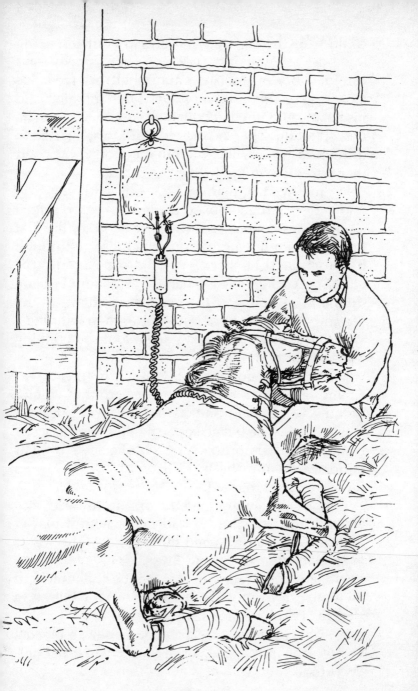

could hear the steady tread of cows outside going towards the milking parlour. Then slowly and carefully Boxer stood up and smelt his feed. He looked very thin and very old at this moment and his coat was stained yellow in places, but at least he was standing. Then he moved a little and started to drink and now William knew the worst was over, that Boxer was going to live.

He followed him round the box with the drip and, after a time, Boxer started to eat his feed slowly like someone wearing false teeth for the first time. William felt a great surge of relief go through him then, and he started to talk to Boxer and the old horse cocked one ear back to listen and William thought this is one of the greatest moments of my life and one of the happiest – better than winning a silver cup, or finding the gang's loot, or winning that last battle.

He realized suddenly how much his head was aching and that no one had seen the wound because of his hair, and he thought, I must get it washed, because it'll go septic if I don't and now he could hear a car approaching – Mr Foxley's car. His father came into the box. "How is he? That's an improvement," he said.

And Mr Foxley untaped the drip from Boxer and covered the opening he had made with a plaster dressing. "We don't need that again. All he wants is good food and rest now," he said.

William was reeling on his feet by this time, but he managed to stretch out a hand to Mr Foxley and to say, "Thank you for saving my horse, sir."

And Mr Foxley said, "You had better go in, son, you look all in. I'll give your father my instructions. Well done."

Indoors there was new bread baking in the oven and his mother waiting to examine his head. He ate and drank and heard his mother's remarks about his wound in a daze of exhaustion. Then he climbed the stairs to his room and each stair was an effort and his bed was the most comfortable bed in the world to his aching body.

Everything is all right, he thought as his head touched the pillow. We *have* won. It was the first time he had dared to think these words and he did not need to touch wood because now it was a fact beyond dispute. He could have sung at this moment if he hadn't been so tired; but his eyes shut almost at once and he fell into instant dreamless sleep.

Chapter Eleven

"I can't believe it's true"

"We're going to be televised and there's a civic welcome in the town hall," said William, sitting on a bale of straw three days later with a bandage round his head.

The holidays were nearly over. Boxer was feeling a little better every day. "We will have to have everyone who was ever in the Patrol," he continued. "The television crew want to do a programme on us and what we have achieved, half here in film on our horses, half live in the studio."

"Oh help!" cried Amanda.

"I'm sure to say the wrong thing," cried Alison, just out of hospital.

"In a way it's goodbye to the Patrol, because the summer holidays are full of shows and Pony Club camp and then there's the start of exam year and you know what that means," said William.

"But goodness, it's exciting," cried Amanda.

"Mum will be pleased; she loves publicity as long as it's good," said Marvin.

"What on earth shall we wear?" asked Natasha.

"Riding clothes for the first bit and what you like

for the civic reception, but I should think skirts for you girls," said Michael.

"And sporty clothes for the interview," added Marvin.

"Trousers and nice shirts, I reckon," said William.

None of them had expected receptions and fame. Everything had happened so fast that they had no time for plans; now the deadline was tomorrow.

"Did you see the bit about us in the *Bidbury Times*? They must have pumped our parents for information. But it's great all the same," said Alison. "It calls us 'this gallant band of young people who are committed to doing good and setting an example to their generation.' It made me blush actually."

"Exactly," agreed Michael.

"As if we weren't doing it for fun," replied Natasha.

They were still feeling limp and incredibly happy after their adventures, rather as one does after competing all day and winning, or after a mammoth long distance ride, or a day's hunting with a twelve mile hack home, but this time it was lasting longer, until William was beginning to wonder if he would ever feel normal again.

They felt very close to one another in friendship, like soldiers who have been through a campaign together, and they felt older than they were and capable of facing anything the future might bring.

They caught the horses and inspected them and decided to bring Mermaid in and wash her so that she looked really clean on television.

"The telly people are coming here tomorrow at ten. They want to film the farmhouse first and me coming out of it with the dogs at my heels; they want to do the whole programme on the Patrol over the last year, not just about the gang, because they can't comment on that until they are judged guilty," said William. "Mum's nearly mad with spring cleaning. They want to interview Dad too, and any of your parents if they'd like to come, just to get their comments on how they felt – and especially your mum's feelings when she was on the train and saw you, Natasha. They say they may only use a quarter of what they shoot, but they plan to be here most of the day and a catering van's coming as well and make-up people – the lot," finished William, thinking that it sounded more like a dream than reality.

"What about the civic reception?" asked Marvin.

"That's in the Town Hall and the mayor's coming and some chief of police," replied William.

"It can't be true. We don't deserve it," cried Amanda.

"It's fantastic, isn't it!" exclaimed Natasha. "We'll never be able to return to normal. We'll be spoilt for ever now."

"I'm going home to tell Mum. She'll be ringing the hairdresser right away and buying herself something to wear and I want to wash Tango and clean her tack. I'll be here at nine tomorrow in case you need help, William. I feel quite dizzy with excitement," cried Amanda.

"I can't believe it's true," cried Alison.

"Nor can I. I must tell Mum at once," said Natasha. "Where did I leave my scooter?"

"Wait for me," cried Michael.

"They may want to film your places too," shouted William. "Warn your parents. Tell them to be ready."

"Mum will be happy at last. All will be forgiven, even Skinflint's windgalls," said Marvin.

They mounted bikes and mopeds and rode away. William walked down to the stable to look at Boxer who was growing stronger. Mr Foxley had been to stitch his wound. He had refused to send a bill. There seemed no end to people's kindness. Mrs Gaze had visited the old couple in the post office which was open again. They had sent William a small silver bowl with a date on it which read 1860.

"What about the others? They were there too," asked William.

"They insisted that you were the captain," replied his mother. "I couldn't persuade them otherwise."

Now she was in curlers, already preparing for the great tomorrow, and his father had bought himself a new pair of boots and Pete had swept the yard better than it had ever been swept before. He was tidying the midden now, and stayed on till nine o'clock making everything shipshape, while William groomed the horses one by one, wondering whether they would want to film them all. Then he brushed the dogs who were completely overcome by such attention as they hadn't been brushed for years. They licked his face and rolled over on their backs and grew sloppier and sloppier.

A few miles away Marvin's mother was helping him to prepare Skinflint for the great day. His windgalls were rubbed with lotion to try to reduce the inflammation, his light chestnut tail and white socks washed and scrubbed, his coat polished until you could see your face in it.

"Nobody will notice how clean he is on television," objected Marvin, his arms aching.

"Of course they will. He must be clean; he'll look so lovely on television," insisted his mother.

She was not bothered about herself or Marvin, only Skinflint seemed to count.

Meanwhile, Amanda's mother rushed to her hairdresser for a special rinse and bought herself new shoes, new make-up and a new dress, while Amanda imagined herself looking fat and awkward and hoped that she could hide behind Tango.

Natasha's mother disappeared towards London in her sports car, muttering that she must have a facial, because her skin was like old leather. Nanny said, "When shall we see it, Natasha? Is it going on tonight?"

"No. It's not live, that comes later," Natasha replied. She had a groom, who polished speckled Checked Princess until her coat shone like newly washed china.

Natasha washed her own hair and her stretch jodhpurs and hoped that the producer was someone famous. She lay on her bed and imagined what she would say when she was interviewed and wished that her brother Leon was with her, instead of in disgrace in Australia. And presently she slept and dreamed that a fabulous producer asked her to meet him at a smart London restaurant.

Michael was not the sort to bother too much about anything. He took life as it came.

"If they're coming here, I'll put my best shirt on," said his father. "Nothing special or new. I'm not poshing up the place for a few telly interviewers

You'd better start riding your horses, Michael. The Royal Windsor Horse Show is less than a month away."

"Right, Dad," replied Michael. "I'll wear my best breeches tomorrow and my black boots, and a shirt. How's that?"

"Fine," said his father. "Now get on your horses and start working."

The whole place smelt of petrol. Michael wondered what the TV crew would make of it when they came. But it didn't matter. Let them see us as we are, he thought. Dad's right; there's no point in polishing the place up.

Alison's mother said, "I can't be there. I'm on duty and I can't change it. Don't say anything silly, Alison. I don't want repercussions." She was on edge and smoking too much. Alison wished that she would marry again. She'll be lost when I'm grown up and gone, she thought. And I'm not sticking round here forever. Next year I can get a job and I shall try to find work at a trekking centre all summer. I'm sick of doing the shopping and the housework. I shall take Rainbow with me. She started to clean her tack and she saw the summer long and golden and herself leading a band of riders through Wales. And she thought, anything's possible in life if you try hard enough. And from now on the sky's the limit as far as I'm concerned.

And she knew suddenly that she had grown up a lot, that she wasn't the same person any more. She washed her hair and went through her books and put some away for her own children when she had them; and she thought, if I don't make university I'll work with horses. I don't care what Mum says.

113

And the future suddenly seemed clear and full of hope.

And now the lights were going out in Deep Wood Farm. William lay in bed listening to an owl calling and he felt happy for the first time in weeks and at this moment, there seemed no end to his happiness. He wondered whether such a feeling was possible unless one had first suffered, like drinking when you are really thirsty or a meal after a time of fasting when water tastes like wine and food like a gift from heaven. A cow was moo-ing in the end field, and he heard Marmaduke neigh, and in the distance a train tore along the railway line. Thinking back, he remembered all that the Patrol had done; he remembered his race across country against the arsonist, the long trudge through floods with the horses, the autistic child who had survived and, last of all, the gang who had lost,and tomorrow will be a new day he thought, with a different sort of battle, a peaceful battle this time.

Chapter Twelve

Fame

They were all at Deep Wood Farm the next morning, clean and shining and full of hope. And the TV team were young and friendly when they came.

They filmed William coming out of the farmhouse with the dogs at his heels and a conversation with all the parents who were there. They filmed the horses which the Patrol had rescued in the autumn grazing fat and round now in the lower meadow, and Boxer with his stable door open and William showing them the wound. They filmed the Patrol on their horses and had a few words with each member. They asked Amanda which was her most exciting moment and she replied without hesitation the moment when she found Tango. They asked Alison about the autistic child and William about the day his barn was burned. They filmed for three hours, talking to everybody about something. Then they filmed each member of the Patrol coming out of his or her own home which took all afternoon. And finally they disappeared to film Maggy, the autistic child the Patrol had rescued, who was being educated in

a special school, and the houses which were burgled and the barn where the loot was found.

Alison kept saying, "I can't believe it's really happening." Marvin's asthma came on because of the excitement and Amanda burst into tears quite suddenly without any reason. Michael remained cool, calm and collected. Natasha chatted up the camera team. William talked about Boxer and refused to discuss himself. Mrs Gaze made up for his modesty by boasting shamelessly about him. It was a day none of them would ever forget.

Two days later they travelled by train for their TV interviews, smartly but casually dressed with butterflies in their stomachs. They chattered and laughed and stared at the flowering countryside and discussed their parents and how impossible they were, and whom they liked in the Pony Club. They had their own dressing-rooms with their names on the doors. They rehearsed everything first and were made up and had their hair done, and drank coffee with the interviewers.

They were each asked a different question. William was asked his worst moment and Michael his best. Amanda was asked whether she was ever afraid and Alison was asked what she had said to Maggy. Natasha was asked why she joined the Patrol and she said that she needed a purpose in life. And Marvin described how it felt to return to a burgled house. None of them dried up, though Amanda said "Um" three times and Marvin coughed, and Alison said, "I'm not sure but I think . . . " In between times the film was shown which had been made two days earlier and they were able to see themselves, and the countryside looking green and fertile and the farmhouse old and romantic. William thought that he looked cross and Amanda whispered that she looked fat and they all hated their voices, and then suddenly it was over. The producer said, "Well done, you were perfect." And the interviewer said, "Terrific," and you could see the tension going out of their faces.

William replied, "Thank you, sir."

And Natasha said, "I sound as though I've got a marble in my mouth. I'm going to take elocution lessons straight away."

"I sound so slow, half-witted in fact," moaned Amanda.

"I wonder what they thought of us watching at home," said Alison.

They rode in a taxi to the station and William longed to be back on the farm with the peace of the countryside all about him.

"It was easier than I thought," said Marvin.

"If only we could have seen it all," replied Michael.

"No thank you, I never want to see myself again," replied Amanda.

"But the horses looked fantastic," cried Alison. "And so did all the houses, except for mine."

"A dog had messed on our path," said Natasha.

"Deep Wood Farm looked the best. It looked fantastic," said Amanda.

"I hope Boxer's all right," said William. "I still have nightmares about him."

"I suppose we wear smart dresses to the reception?" asked Alison.

"Yes, or skirts I should think. I'm wearing a velvet jacket," replied Michael.

"I'm wearing Grandpa's smoking jacket," said William.

"Dad's going to lend me something," added Marvin.

"I shall have to make something out of a curtain," said Alison. "I haven't any money left."

"My mother will lend you something. Come to our place tomorrow," answered Natasha, "and we will have a trying on session. You look the same size."

"I can't. I can't wear your mother's things."

"Why not, does she have such bad taste?" asked Natasha, laughing.

"You know I don't mean that," replied Alison. "It just seems a cheek, that's all."

"Don't be idiotic. I'll expect you at ten a.m. without fail," replied Natasha.

"I've got a hideous skirt," said Amanda. "But it doesn't matter beause I look awful in everything."

They could see their home station now, lit up, with people waiting for their train. Parents rushed to meet them, congratulating them, making Alison squirm and Amanda blush. They were bundled into cars and driven away into the night, and another day was suddenly over.

"What a day it's been," cried Mrs Gaze. "I never thought I should live to see the like of it."

"Did I look all right, Amanda?" asked her mother.

"Great," said Amanda, "But the horses looked even better."

"You couldn't see Skinflint's windgalls, I looked specially," said Marvin's mother. "I thought he looked the best turned out of all the horses. Didn't you?"

119

"I don't know," answered Marvin, wondering why his mother always turned everything into a competition.

"I should have brought the old Rolls for you, Michael," his dad said. "You're really quite a star now."

"I wish you had tied back your hair, Alison," said her mother who had an obsession with neatness. "Otherwise you looked a treat."

Natasha's mother threw her arms round her neck. "You were gorgeous," she cried. "Absolutely gorgeous; and we've had a letter from Leon and he's doing very well. Isn't that lovely?"

"Yes, terrific. Can you lend Alison a dress, Mum?" asked Natasha.

"Yes, of course, when is she coming?"

"Tomorrow at ten o'clock."

"My skirt won't do up. Help!" shrieked Amanda the next evening. "And I've got to meet the others at the crossroads at seven thirty. I told you I was getting fatter. It's all those cakes you keep making, Mum, it isn't fair."

"Hold your tummy in," replied her mother. "Don't breathe. The zip's moving." Amanda had had her hair done at the hairdressers. She was very nervous. She had her invitation card in her hand. It read:

> "Your company is requested at The Town Hall
> for a reception in honour of The Pony Patrol."

It was in gilt lettering and also said Supper and Drinks in one corner and Formal Dress in another and R.S.V.P. to the Town Clerk somewhere else.

Just looking at it made Amanda feel nervous.

Mrs Gaze had spent a lot of time mending and

pressing William's grandfather's old smoking jacket, because he refused to wear anything else.

Now he was trying to tie a black tie in front of the bathroom mirror, thinking that it was harder than a hunting tie, but glad that it was black instead of white and wouldn't show finger marks.

He wished he could take Boxer with him. His invitation was in his breast pocket. He felt very strange, but not frightened, only nervous that he wouldn't address the mayor in the right way or would use the wrong knife and fork.

Marvin was wearing his father's dinner jacket. The sleeves were rather long and didn't show the gold cuff links he had also borrowed. He had swallowed a tablet to keep his asthma at bay and he felt rather drowsy.

Natasha's mother was helping Alison. She had lent her a dress and now she was clipping a single strand of pearls round her neck.

"This is one of the greatest moments of your life. You must look your best, darling," she said. "Now for perfume. What would you like?"

Natasha wore a green dress which matched her green eyes and set off her red hair.

Michael was wearing his father's dinner jacket and trousers.

"I look a fool," he said. "And just look at my hair. I look really stupid. Must I wear all this, Dad? Can't I just go in hunting kit?"

"Not to a reception."

"I wish we had never been asked," said Michael.

A wagon with two shire horses waited for them at the crossroads. A placard across read THE PONY PATROL and there were flags draped on the sides.

"This can't be for us," cried Amanda when she

121

saw it. "We don't deserve it."

"Exactly," said Michael.

Marvin's father took out his camera. They climbed up the steps at the back. Amanda nearly tripped over her skirt. Alison was terrified of spoiling her dress. Natasha was laughing. William waited for the girls to get inside. He wondered what he would say at dinner. As they travelled through the town, crowds came out to cheer them.

"We're like a football team," said Michael.

"I feel silly," said Martin.

"We don't deserve it," cried Amanda again.

"We did nothing special," said Alison, wiping her eyes.

"I can't believe it's happening," said Amanda.

People clapped as they neared the Town Hall and a man shouted "Bravo". Children ran forward to pat the horses, cameras flashed.

"Smile," said William. "Keep smiling."

He couldn't believe it was happening either, that he, William Gaze, was riding through the town in a wagon, being cheered.

"We'll be spoilt for ever after this," cried Alison.

"We don't deserve it," said Amanda for the third time.

Inside the dignitaries of the small town were drinking cocktails. They made way for the Patrol. The mayor shook their hands.

"Pleased to meet you, sir," said William.

"Hullo," said Michael.

"How do you do," said Amanda.

"Hi," said Natasha.

"Good evening, sir," said Marvin.

"Pleased to meet you," whispered Alison, imitating William.

122

They sat down to dinner and the mayor made a long speech. None of them could think of it afterwards without blushing. It was full of words like dedicated and it ended with the reading of a poem by Rudyard Kipling called *If*. Later everyone sang *For They Are Jolly Good Fellows*, raised their glasses and shouted "To the Pony Patrol". Later still the police chief presented them with certificates of bravery and a man in a suit gave them a cheque and called it a Reward.

Then there were cries of SPEECH until William stepped forward and said, "We are honoured to be here. What we did anyone else would have done given the chance," and people stamped their feet and cried, "Nonsense" and "Not true".

And he continued, "We did it for ourselves too or most of it, for the safety of our houses and barns."

And someone shouted, "Nonsense. What about the old couple and the little girl?"

And William said, "We just did our best," and sat down, and there were more cheers. Marvin was feeling unsteady on his feet by this time and they were all exhausted by emotion. Coffee was served and now the lights were on outside in the town; and then suddenly someone said, "The Queen," and there was a rolling of drums and they all stood up straight and sang "*God Save the Queen*".

And William thought, thank goodness it's over.

Natasha wanted it to last for ever. Alison was pleased that she hadn't spoilt Mrs Merriot's dress, and Michael was longing to get out of his father's dinner jacket . . . Masses of people surged forward to shake their hands and William knew suddenly now that he would hate real fame. I would hate to be recognized wherever I went, he thought, to be stared at and asked for autographs.

The night was cool and clear when they stepped outside. The shire horses had gone. Instead their parents waited in ordinary clothes, standing by ordinary cars.

The Patrol stood on the steps and looked at each other and then Alison and Amanda both kissed William at the same time, and Michael kissed Natasha very quickly and Alison kissed Marvin because he looked left out. Then Natasha said, "This is Old Lang Syne, isn't it?"

And William replied, "I don't know, but I want to be quiet for a week or two, to relax and look after my stud of horses."

Their parents were crowding round now, saying, "How was it? What happened?" And William said, "Someone gave us a cheque for one hundred pounds. I don't know what we're meant to do with it."

And Amanda declared, "We'll have to have a meeting then."

"Yes," cried Alison.

"Of course," said Michael.

"So it's not goodbye," cried Natasha.

"It's never goodbye," said William. "Not as long as I'm here, and the farm's here. Deluges of past blood and tears bind us together, and there's sure to be another day when we're needed."

He got into his father's battered car and the sky was full of a million stars now, and he thought life goes on, the good and the bad, hope and despair, nothing alters that.

PONY PATROL

The Pony Patrol – a team of young riders whose sworn aim is to patrol the countryside on horseback, watching, searching and protecting the peace of the land.

Follow the adventures of the Pony Patrol riders in Christine Pullein-Thompson's gripping series of books.

Pony Patrol	£2.99 ☐
Pony Patrol S.O.S.	£2.99 ☐
Pony Patrol Fights Back	£2.99 ☐
Pony Patrol and the Mystery Horse	£2.99 ☐

All Simon & Schuster Young Books are available at your local bookshop or can be ordered direct from the publisher. Just tick the titles you want and fill in the form below. Prices and availability subject to change without notice.

Simon & Schuster Cash Sales Department, PO Box 11, Falmouth, Cornwall, TR10 9EN, England.

Please enclose a cheque or postal order to the value of the cover price and allow the following for postage and packing:
UK: 80p for the first book, and 20p for each additional book ordered up to a maximum charge of £12.
BFPO: 80p for the first book, and 20p for each additional book.
OVERSEAS & EIRE: £1.50 for the first book, £1.00 for the second book, and 30p for each subsequent book.

Name ....

Address ....

....

Postcode ....